G000162012

"With its forceful, elegant prose and unblinking h. ..., GEESE SEE GOD reminded me on every page of the work of Dennis Lehane and Cormac McCarthy, two writers I greatly admire. The characters here, utterly original and deftly if lightly interlaced, wander the bright halls of love and connection, and plumb the dark depths of religious fanaticism, troubled sexuality, and violence. There are disturbing scenes in abundance, but Hearon always stops short of despair and the gratuitous; always there is a mystical twinkling, a magical turn of phrase, a splash of poetry, a glimmer of hope, a redemptive moment. I enjoyed every word."

ROLAND MERULLO

author of 24 books, including

Breakfast with Buddha and The Revere Beach Trilogy

"The best portal to *DO GEESE SEE GOD* is a map of surrender: no signposts, no boundaries, only the glorious invitation to fall and believe and be. Allow the pieces of this fractured family saga to sing to you. These are the voices of siblings and parents, of minders and ghosts, and within this dark vortex are the everyday fierce desires and laments we all know—a story that will move you in ways you won't expect. In weaving this gorgeously written tornado, Todd Hearon has created an epic that lingers in the secret corners of our complicated hearts."

ANNE SANOW

author of *Triple Time*

"Todd Hearon's *DO GEESE SEE GOD* is wild, ferocious, vulnerable—a deep song that beautifully captures loss and loneliness with hilarity and precision. Read it for its big-hearted characters; read it for the voice that embraces you, speaks to you, and takes you in. A wonderful debut."

PAUL YOON

author of *Snow Hunters, Once the Shore* and *The Mountain*

ALSO BY TODD HEARON

POETRY

Strange Land

No Other Gods

Crows in Eden

DO GEESE SEE GOD

DO GEESE SEE GOD

TODD HEARON

NEUTRAL ZONES PRESS

2021

DO GEESE SEE GOD
By Todd Hearon
© 2021 by Todd Hearon

Published by Neutral Zones Press
Brooklyn
neutralzonespress.com

Cover and text design by adam b. bohannon

For any information,
please address Neutral Zones Press: editor.neutralzonespress.com

ISBN: 978-0-578-30521-9 (pb)
ISBN: 978-0-578-31636-9 (ebook)

This is a work of fiction. Names, characters, businesses, places,
events, locales, and incidents are either the products of the author's
imagination or used in a fictitious manner.

ACKNOWLEDGEMENTS

I am grateful for a fellowship from Dartmouth College and The Frost Place, during which time a portion of this manuscript was completed. Thanks to those who read it at various stages and offered their encouragement, guidance and support—Mary Hubbell, Greg Brown, Anne Sanow, Paul Yoon, Tanya Waterman, Roland Merullo—and to Dan Falatko for his faith-made-fact.

"Stranger, the ways of dreams are fickle and perplexing,

   And not everything we humans dream comes true

   Because of the doors, the two doors, through which dreams enter,

   The one carved from ivory and the one of polished horns.

   Those dreams that pass the threshold of the tusks

   Deceive and come to nothing in the end,

   And those that come winding through the antlers' crowns

   Come true, to those of us able to discern them.

   But surely my nightmare didn't come from there."

Odyssey, XIX, 560-569

CONTENTS

DO GEESE SEE GOD

THE DREAM OF ONE

+

It is the tendency of shit in fucked-up lives to snowball. *The worst is not, so long as we can say, This is the worst.* As Father always said. If the law of eternal recurrence is true, and the sins of the parents are multiplied and heaped upon the heads of the children, there's no escaping clean; all heroic gestures of resistance or resilience can be sized up in the ant's ability to withstand the avalanche. There's one cold comfort you can take as you're swept under: the two of you, your shadow and yourself, were holding hands.

I trace the origin of our long line of fuck-ups—Carrie's and mine—to the death of our parents in a car crash on the highway near Ithaca, New York, when we were eight. That's a convenient, if arbitrary, marker. It might have started long before—probably did, after a series of botched in vitro, at the unlikely moment of conception when we entered the wings of the world as separate eggs. Or when, the story goes, we emerged blue from the birth canal tangled in each other's umbilicals. *Why did it not end there?* A lovers' pact—preemptory, redemptive—in the lion's mouth of the waiting world. They had to cut our cords from around the other's throat.

For better and for worse, from that point we were inseparable. If not one flesh, one intelligence and spirit. I could predict when she would walk into a room. She knew—and would tell me in the morning—

3

what I'd dreamed. So all those years that we were physically apart never felt to me like distance. She was always there, in that inward space I'd made for us of memory and lost potential, I the wandering soul and she the fixed and certain star. It's probably why, when I found her again, my long in-oh-so-many-ways-lost twin, it felt, in some strange cosmic way, directed. Like destiny, or a doom you willingly put on because it is your own.

It was near Buffalo. Or somewhere. Maybe Syracuse. Or Rome. Or Ilion. Those old New York names, the debris of antiquity hauled from its sarcophagi and reimagined in calcite and titanium. Which, Father said, would outlast time, though I never understood the utility of that. A hot June night. I had come in late, having driven all day and most of the night before, the semi light, on return to the company in Albany. Sick of the road, sick of the heat, sick of Cassandra's smell in the berth. There were never any rooms on the highway at that hour, but I found a sign lit up on a spur a couple of miles over, a swaybacked joint with weekly/monthly rates. FREE ADULT ENTERTAINMENT flickered in red neon like a desperate, spastic dancer.

I don't ascribe it to coincidence that I was handed a greasy key with 216 on the ring, my birthday. Or that, when I turned the TV on and fell back on the bed, the entertainment was hot underway. I was too weary to get up—or is that just what I tell myself? Be honest, Benjie. In the loneliness and poverty of my life, I felt compelled to watch.

There is something about two naked bodies struggling to fuse—and, in pornography, attempting a third merger with the viewer, you—that I find unspeakably sad. It is so human in its hell-bent fluster to achieve what can never humanly be had: the dream of one. And the sadness so much sadder when the desperation's being played, when it's a sham. I lay there for a long time, despite my need for sleep, trying to imagine the people in the screen *as* people. As daughters. Sons. Maybe even mothers and fathers. (Maybe even, by some impossible chance, actual lovers.) Real people with real lives outside the screen that they'd step into after like a clean set of clothes, have a bowl of Cheerios and begin the day. People I might actually meet in my life. And then, as always, it seemed so sad, these things we're stripped to, these bodies, these camera-cut appendages and torsos severed on display as at a butcher's counter. Nothing but quivering, thrusting cuts of meat. And I felt myself in my weakness, in my own diminished state, becoming drawn to the appendages and torsos, to their sculpted angularities and soft, inviting curves. And I thought, *God, why not, if this is all there is?* Nothing but the play, the appearances of passion. Nothing but the pixilated forms that love or passion takes, so cruelly limited by these bodies that give the passion form. And then I gave myself, in fantasy, over to them, and I entered—I allowed myself to enter—their luminous adjacent room. And I stood inside the screen and watched the pixel people play, a bundle of pixels now myself slimed with their secretions, for what seemed an eternal sleep until I woke.

The sun was strong, shining through the cracks in the blinds. I cursed myself and rolled onto my side and stared for a long time at the slender blinding bars that meant life. The TV was still on, but muted as I'd had it. I rose to shut it off and stopped. On the screen, in a pose of theatric degradation, eyes trained on me, on anyone, mouth open in an attitude of agony and hunger, my sister, Carrie, played. No mistaking—though more than fourteen years had passed since I had seen her—no mistaking those eyes I knew, even at their most seductive, to be a mockery (how many times as a child I'd seen that same expression in our games, heard her voice *pretty, pretty please* promising to love me always, always just to coax whatever coveted possession from my grasp and, after, to whiplash into icy triumph). And as her face turned, now, to the unseen face thin-lipped with straining over her, its body rocking hers with all its terrible force, and the tight thighs lifted and her red mouth opened into little imagined gasps and cries ("please" again, and "please, please, pretty please"), I took my hand from where it had inadvertently fallen to my shrunken groin and reached and stopped the agitated screen.

I never went to Albany that morning. I took the truck and headed south for New York City where I knew with all a snowball's chance in Hell (I knew) I'd find her. My lost shadow. My severed secondself. Soiled star . . .

So sang my soul against the avalanche—

+

Two things they never tell you when you're waiting to get into this trainfuck of a world:

1. Only brains can save you.

2. Brains are not enough.

Take him. Smartest person I ever knew in my life, by far, talk about brains, he was *born* one hopped-up blubbering brain. Sign-languaged his ABCs, the whole freaking alphabet, when he was one, was reading the dictionary by the time he was five. He read *the dictionary.* What kid does that? But brains as in sense of direction? Common sense? Might as well have been talking to an amoeba. He'd get lost in a toy box with a GPS. That was me, the GPS, I was the wheels to carry the brain around, the big sister who'd sweep in at the last rail-screeching second to save him from whatever crap-assed concoction he was cooking up in that cauldron of noodles of his. Well. Till the end at least. But that's another story. And besides, we're not talking here of me.

But you need brains. And by God he had 'em.

But brains are not enough.

I'll tell you a story, this professor runs into a crackhead in an alley one night as he's coming home from work. It's dark so he can't see the guy, he just hears the voice, "Say, Wiseman, what's the secret of life?" And the professor, being a high-level brainy dude, a real Einstein, he goes into this elaborate spiel about Ultimate Human Happiness and the union of body and mind and some New-Age seven-chakras shit and there's a *pop!* and the top of his head comes flying off. And the crackhead reaches down, pulls out the dead guy's wallet and says, "The secret of life, Bozo, is keep the fuck out of dark alleys at night." Right? That's all I'm saying.

Our mother was a professor, talk about brains. Real bigwig, taught history of philosophy at Cornell. Not that that means anything now. (*Pop!*) And you'd think, you'd really think—even after that, the death of the two people responsible for getting you onto this shithole of a planet—you'd think it'd be something you might be able to get over after something like, what?—eighteen years. But not him. Not the amoeba. For him, from the beginning, it was like some gigantic hemorrhoid erupting in the cosmos, some crowbar in the sky sent down to peel the ceiling of certainty and security off our lives. Granted, we were six. But *things happen.* And not always (I would constantly have to tell him) for some Higher Purpose. Not like pain or suffering mean shit outside themselves. Not like they're supposed to teach us anything. *Life* is pain. Pain, if anything, just tells us we're alive. And while we're alive we can give the big Fuck You back to pain.

But not him. He collected pain, he cultivated it, built a personal philosophy of pain, and through it fooled himself into believing it had a purpose. That it was part of a Greater Plan, that it "adhered" (his favorite word), that it pointed somewhere. Which "presupposed" (another favorite) that it had somewhere to start. And then we were back to that

dumbass falling-dominos game he would always play—tracing all of our
so-called misery back to a source, which for him probably stretched back
to the first poor finless fucker washed up naked on the shore of the
world. Which released *him* (do you see it?) from any responsibility. When
if you really wanted to see it how it was, you only had to go back as far
as when he pulled that shitheaded stunt at age eleven that landed him in
juvie for the next seven years of our life *and* which began—if we want
to see it his way—in my humble opinion our whole fucked-up history
of misery meant to teach us Absolutely Nothing.

We were living in foster care at the time, wards of The Great State
of New York, as no other relative had found it convenient to be alive
or "emotionally viable" after our parents' death. (Aunt Emma: that's
another story.) He had this friend, a little fuck-eyed freckled weed of a
kid named Rudy, older than him, probably thirteen. They used to play
mad scientist together. Strapping lightning rods to roadkill, or wir-
ing them up to car batteries, making the muscles twitch. Real swanky
Frankensteiny stuff. One day, Fuck-eye decides he's going to steal his
parents' car. He's got a plan. They're gonna drive out to the interstate
and firebomb stopped cars. Which involved, as the plan hopped into
practice, bombing stopped *cop* cars who'd stopped the other stopped
cars. Get it? Right. What did I tell you? Shit for common sense. At least
they had the brains—or just the good bad luck—to bomb a cop car
with no cop in it. Cop's standing at the other car's passenger window,
green sedan tears by and a skinny arm (guess whose?) swings a Molotov
cocktail under the gas tank. *KA-BOOM!* Fucker blows to high heaven.
Passengers in the other car got out all right, but the cop gets burned
real bad all over, he's in the hospital for something like the next three
months, and when they pull the bandages off his eyes he can't see. They
might have gotten away with it, but Fuck-eye's folks were standing in
the yard when they got home. Story's on the news that night—eye

witnesses, green sedan . . . Bingo. Didn't sit so well with t
the parents brought them in. Benj got seven years. Fuck-(
know's still doing time.

Got sent to that detention center over in Lansing. Oh, the stories
he told me later about that place. It's all under investigation now, high
time, little too late. The guards . . . Those fuckers were brutal. Broken
arms, broken teeth, that wasn't the half of it. Do you know—this was
all in the news after—during the time he was there, that place alone
was responsible for something like five percent of the psychotropic
drugs purchased in the entire state of New York? That's what?—like
more than a million pills, 600 a day or some shit like that given to 120
boys over seven years' time? All experimental, off-the-market stuff, they
dished it out like candy, as "chemical restraint." Just kept 'em constantly
drugged, beat the hell out of 'em if they refused to take it. Well you
know what that'll do to a kid over time. Or maybe you don't. And the
other boys. I won't even go into that. You can imagine them getting
ahold of someone like him. Skinny white boy, suburban sheltered life.
Let's just say they got *real* creative. And the guards, once they got whiff
of what he'd done to land himself in there—maiming one of their
own—they took a personal pleasure in tormenting him. It wasn't all
just physical. When they saw how much he loved books—how much
he needed books—they started keeping them from him. Can you believe it? Books, for fuck's sake. He'd have to sneak them in from the
other boys, for "favors." And when the guards would find them, as they
always would, hidden of course in the most obvious places, oh the
beatings they'd give him then. *With* the books. Later, years later, after
the old regime rolled over, he finally got to use the library, to finish his
GED. And get this. One of the fuckers still around from when he first
arrived, he would wait for him in the stacks when he knew he'd be
alone and make him give him blow jobs while he—the guard—read

to him out loud from whatever book he was working on. "Cost of an education, kid," he'd tell him.

So let's just say his whole experience in the care of the wonderful Empire State was a little short of what you'd call Candyland. But you've gotta give him credit. Life, it fucked him over good, but he didn't just lie down like a dog and die. He went somewhere with it. Well. He went to trucker school. Got his commercial license, learned to drive the big rigs. And the years from when he got out of Lansing till he turned twenty-one—when the company moved him up to interstate—those were the years he spent hauling chickens back and forth over the highways that, in his mind, had formed his fate. Taken his parents, taken his childhood, taken him away from me. He had a lot of room for thinking in that time, in that book-crammed, drugged-out, haunted brain of his. Talking to himself—or talking to his sidekick, that crazy inflatable doll, Cassandra (that's another story). But I know one thing he never thought about. Because he only learned of it years later. He never thought about the private little hell that fucking firebomb landed *me* in. Foster home, girl alone, having her twat ransacked at night. So that's why when *I* line up the dominos, they stretch back not to some wreck on the highway in 1993 and the death of two people I don't (to be completely honest) even remember clearly, but to an act of stupidity—*fuck-brained* stupidity—whose consequences still keep me up at night.

But like I said, we're not talking here of me.

And anyway, it wasn't in the amoeba's hardware to think about consequences, or to take responsibility. No. I take that back. He did, in the end. By God he did. The way that final shit went down . . . "Epic," to use one of his favorite words. It's just too bad the epic end was a wee bit fucking late. I always told him, *Benjie, the only point of living is to stay alive.*

+

If there's a door at the end of a hall, there is a hall. If there's a hall will be a structure to contain it. *The blueprint, Father said, is the soul towards which the structure strives, as flesh aspires to spirit, world to word, material to mind. The work of the world is return, a transmutation of physical appearances into ideal form.* If there's a window at the light end looking down must be stairs. If there are stairs that lead to a counter with a buzzer and a bearded woman behind the glass, will I be let in? (But only if she's sleeping.) Behind the winter's glass, the mother grizzly sleeps, waking with her uncomprehending young to trundle to the ocean. Migratory patterns in the blood of the mind, in the bone of memory not entirely yours. A salmon-sense of smell—magnetoreceptive—returning up new rivers to its natal ground. (Beware the grizzly's maw.) Geese hurtling through corridors of air, flyways five thousand abstract miles, to light upon ancestral breeding grounds. Nothing in Earth is lost. Be what the aborigine knows: Earth is Intelligence, is Information, and the blood of the gods circulates its current through the unseen, subterranean veins. Geomancy. Follow the vital flow to the mouth where the myth perennially takes place. Listen for the songline. Sing the forgotten world into existence.

All the myths, Father said, all the old stories, play out in our blood, and in one lifetime we are many lives. Electra and Orestes at the sacrifice. Orpheus and Eurydice ascending. Oedipus. Odysseus. All has been told before, all has been accomplished, and will occur again, not once but an infinite number of times. Time is the womb in the eternal mother where our immutable permutations play. If it seems that we've been here before, it's because we've never been away.

She opened the door.

"Doesn't that make it all pretty pointless?"

"Only if you believe it's pointless now," I said.

+

My shadow with no body. No body but a shadow. That's what I was thinking when I turned at the top of the stairs and saw him, standing in the sickly yellow-green light of the hall a few doors down. I just stood there and looked at him—he was staring at the floor, he didn't seem to sense me—watching him for a long time waver in and then back out of existence. As if he'd always been there. As if he'd never been.

He was leaning against the wall, the smoky coil from a cigarette snaking up along his arm. Unbuttoned flannel shirt, an A-frame draped across his sunken chest; blue jeans gone black at the knees and thighs with grime. Long, greasy hair, his eyes and face in shadow, beneath the brim of a ridiculous green trapper's hat. I thought of someone, somebody in a story, washed up on some long-forgotten desert isle. That worn away. That whittled. He looked like he hadn't eaten in weeks.

And then he spoke—a thin, dry voice: "How are you Carrie"—and I felt my pulse again, first in the sides of my head, then behind my eyes, then down along my throat and into my chest. Part of me wanted to rush to him, take him in my arms and squeeze the space out of the space between us as if no time in all the world had ever passed. And another part of me wanted to kill him.

But how can you kill someone who's already been dead for fourteen years?

He lifted his face and looked at me. His eyes . . . Not only that I knew them as nearly as I knew my own, not only that they'd seen inside me deeper than anybody's eyes had ever seen (not only that they looked that deeply now)—they were like warped and fractured stars, crazy with something I saw in that moment I could never truly know. And I felt again the swell and sweep of all the life between us.

I started down the hall. He took a final drag off the butt and twisted the cherry off the tip. It fell to the carpet where he ground it with the toe of a new white tennis shoe. A kid's . . . As I passed him he bent and picked up a brown paper bag and followed me like a stray kitten to the door.

"Bet you're wonderin' how I found ya." His voice—it sounded strangely off—higher than I remembered, and tinny, almost mechanical.

"No," I said. I'm sure I was visibly shaking. I could hardly manage the handful of keys and my breath was short and hot.

"432," he said and held up a key, my spare. "In the crack behind the mailbox." Then, with a weird little singsong: "*As predicted* . . . " There was a deep scar running along his jaw under the stubble, coming up to the crack in his lips then jagging back across his cheek in a Joker kind of smile. But the eyes weren't smiling. Little haunted holes. I shoved the key into the bolt, pushed hard and almost fell into the room—

She opened the door.

I could see she had been crying. She took my hands and brought me into the pinkwhite cushioned room, sat me down next to her on the bed and laid her head in my lap, beginning to cry again. "How can I be in this life without you?" Her body was shaking, her fists white flowers on my knee. I laid my hands on her head and raised her face to mine. Her eyes, aswim with little Christmas lights, dark wells of understanding.

> *Look for me in the secret place*
> *Beneath the stars in darkness drifting*
> *Where moonlight speaks a language of the face*
> *And thought's a firefly lifting*

I kissed her on the forehead. Only once, only there. As Plato kissed, the poets say: a quarter-inch from the brain.

Take this kiss upon thy brow
And in parting from you now

She sat on the sofa and began to rummage through her bag. She pulled out a joint and lit it, shaking. Draw, draw. One two, one two. *I carried your heart with me. I carried it in my heart*

Carrie, I said—

He sat on the sofa and lifted the paper bag and opened it and pulled out a stack of letters, tied with an old gray shoelace. *See?* Pink envelopes, from a lifetime ago; a girl's loopy cursive; on the top, in the bottom corner, two little fairy stickers. I felt my stomach turn to ice. Every one from me. All from his time at Lansing. Every single one of them still unopened.

I carried your heart

I could have clawed out his eyes.

But so I saw it then, he never knew.

+

When our father was a young man, after finishing his degrees, he took a job for a time with a firm in New York City. His first building, bold with the so-called "innovative design" which would later win him his many accolades and awards, was The Center for the Cultivation of Mind and Spirit, in lower Manhattan, near Battery Park. Tall, diaphanous panels split with glass; soaring balustrades and cables; the inside like a ship of air and light—meant to reflect the Center's purpose and philosophy: intelligential sweep aligned with pneumatic scope, superabounding the merely corporeal constraints of money and materials; all anchored by the architect's twin aims: functionality and security for the building's future occupants.

He also, it happens, designed the house where all of us lived until the two of them were killed.

When you visit that first building now, as we two now have, you find an exercise palace. On every tier, facing huge illumined panes or staring into agitated screens, people run, going nowhere, heaving cables and foam-covered pipes, an infinitely replicated architectonics of gleaming, sculpted flesh. A poignant illustration, I have thought, of the death of a vision and the afterlife of its shell. A structure, used in a way it had never been intended. And the people who inhabit it who never knew.

Carrie, I said. It's like us.

It is, she said. And now you know.

I'll kill him, I said. She looked at me and rolled her eyes.

Like I could let you do that all alone.

+

Of course, it didn't help that the tractor-trailer was basically stolen, off the company radar now for something like seven days. So the state troopers are already on the prowl.

And it didn't help that when we got back to Ithaca, the house was no longer there. (But in the Age of Information, everyone leaves a trail.)

They were living in a retirement community. The plan was to break in at night while they were sleeping, tie the old woman up—not that she didn't deserve a good braining, too, the crazy bearded bitch, like living in a fucking freakshow in that house—it was old man Zyklos we were after. It was funny, the whole time we talked about it, or while I talked about it, he didn't say a word for a long, long time, just sat there staring at the wall—how it started just after he was taken away and went on till I was thirteen—when I guess my body ceased to interest him, the fucker—the whole time I had this feeling I was talking about someone else *to* someone else who'd never even existed. Or maybe some other person that maybe I might have known, in another lifetime, a lifetime ago. Well. It *was* another lifetime. Right? Another person, another body some old fat gray fucker groped and poked away.

He just sat there, my letters in his hand, slowly clenching and unclenching his fingers around them. *Not that reading them would have helped. Not that you could have done anything.* His jaw was clenched and the long scar on his cheek was quivering.

At fifteen I ran, I told him, never went back. Came here, got into acting. Not what you think, I said. I had high aspirations. I still had some dreams. Besides, in the City you can become anybody, right? He lifted his eyes briefly, then let them fall back to the floor. But at the end of that first summer, I found myself living in a homeless shelter. And word on the street was there was cash for video porn. I'm just saying. When you're fifteen and hard-up and hungry enough you'll do a lot.

And besides, like I said, it was just another body.

That fall the Towers fell. It seemed a sign.

I don't care what you've done, he said. I don't care what happens. I only want to be with you.

And then he asked, Are you sure?

And I said yes. But I don't think then I really thought we would actually kill anyone. I don't think I thought about what killing someone means. I thought, I don't know, we might just remind them we were still here, still out in the world, maybe just give them a big scare. Right? We were kids, twenty-somethings, still just as lost as ever. I guess, in the absence of everything else, it just seemed a thing to do. Get back somehow—stupid as it sounds—to where we started. Try to wipe out all the shit of the years between. Start clean somehow. Somehow start new.

But mostly I thought I didn't want to lose him again. No matter what. I only wanted to be with him, too.

Which is a pretty fucked-up reason for getting a person killed.

But it's true.

So anyway. We've got a plan. We find the house. We stake it out, the three of us, him and me and Cassandra. Which gives us a couple of days to take some strolls down Nightmare Lane. Past the old firebomb spot, past the spot on the highway where the parents got smeared. All warm and fuzzy Norman Rockwell shit. Past the old house where the four of us used to live . . . There was a family living there now, with kids. And more new houses behind it where there used to be a field. (*Remember that stream in the tall grass where we'd catch salamanders?*)

We sat in the truck for a long time, quiet, watching the stranger children playing.

And was any of it, was any of it at all, any of it true? These stories we tell ourselves, the stories we find ourselves inside, like air inside the rainbowed magic bubbles we used to blow inside that very imagined field, so also doomed? Was there ever a time my father put me on his lap in a bright gold minivan and let me steer? Or impossibly my mother gathering apples in an upstate orchard? So high, so high into the branches we were lifted, and the smell of the apples and the wasps droning over our heads. One stung you on the eye so you remember. (But not the grassy world before or after)

That night he asked me if there was any of it I believed.

What, I said, like none of it ever happened?

Who cares if it happened. Just, is there any of it you believe?

He was lying with his head in my lap, staring up at the stars. We'd parked the truck out by a campground near the lake.

I have the memory, Dumbshit. Doesn't that mean it happened?

You have the *story*, he said. He was trying to get all deep. Pass me the joint, I told him.

The memory is the soul. The story is its body. Or something like that was what he finally said.

We smoked on that one for a while.

I don't know shit about souls, I told him.

Then he said, *Memory is the punishment for being in a body.*

He rolled his head sideways in my lap, looking out at the dark. And I looked at his half-face, at the scar that crawled like a highway over his cheek.

Tell me, I said, running my finger along it.

And when he tried to speak it came out as a cry.

+

When I lay there at night and would feel them in me, with every flash flash flash of pain—hearing their animal sounds above, listening to both of our cries—I would think of the honking of geese high overhead, hurtling through the dark, wild and untouchable, disembodied voices, far echoes of us in flight. And I'd think of the four of us standing together in the field behind the house one autumn evening. Mother, her hands on our shoulders, saying, Listen. Close your eyes. And I felt the world peel back as they swept over. And something in me lifted, also seeking flight. And as they passed out of hearing and the room came back, bright walls, small, with only human voices, and the pain returned, I'd think, Pain. Pain is the punishment for being in a body.

It's the same. It's the same thing, Carrie, I said.

+

So the night of the thing arrives.

Doomed from the beginning, I can see that now. The gods were against us.

She was sitting on the sofa in the dark watching TV when we came in. Strike one.

But I just keep thinking, keep replaying it in my mind, we could have got it right, we could have carried it off.

Maybe. If it hadn't been for that cat.

That motherfucking cat.

It was sitting up on the back of the sofa, wide-eyed, head cocked, as we came in behind her from the kitchen. It was watching us—or sort of watching in our general direction because I'm sure the thing was blind. Moon eyes, milky white—in the backlight of the TV sort of glowing—and the body just a sack of skin and bones, with clumps of white fur sticking out in jagged patches. Ghostly white, spookily still. And its moon eyes blindly watching us. Like the guardian of an Egyptian tomb, he later said. I'm sneaking up behind her with the bat, this big Fred-Flintstone aluminum number he kept in the truck, back in the sleeping berth, "for thieves," he said. Which I thought was kind of funny. What, I asked, you scared someone's gonna make off with your inflatable honey? He just reached back, patted an old Army-issue duffle he kept tucked down beside the mattress. You'll see, Carrie, he said.

But the cat.

The weird thing just keeps watching me. Sitting up, frozen behind her on the sofa with its white head sort of brainlessly cocked, and a little fucked-up twisted smile. It's freaking me out, those eyes, like empty marbles, and the smile now, like some kind of dare, I think—like it's daring me, daring me to whack it. And why not? I think. Let's really tear things up. Scare the old bitch shitless. I raise the bat. And I'm coming in for the swing. Closer, closer, almost there—. And then it hits me. Wait a second. I *know* that cat. That's fucking Snowball, my old kitten.

I'm standing there with the bat in the air. And the brainless thing's just smiling at me. My brain starts doing some seriously fucked-up things. It's been like how many years? But it's all coming back. I'm in a white Easter dress, and she's talking to me about my period, how *you're a grown girl now, and you need to be aware.* Aware of what? I wanna ask. His cock in my mouth? His smell under my skin and I can't pray it out? *Your body is the temple of the Lord,* she says. *Pray without ceasing.* So I'm praying, without ceasing, in my pink bed now with Snowball down between my legs 'cause that's where he likes to pet her saying, *Nice kitty, nice, nice . . .* Seriously fucked up shit, that's what I'm saying. Then I hear this loud *cluh-clang!* and the room comes back. And I'm still standing there, and she's sitting on the couch like nothing, none of it, ever happened. And nothing *has* happened, not yet. Except I look at my feet and I've dropped the fucking bat.

She turned her head.

Her yellow eye like a turtle's, fixed on me, on us, shot through with terror, trying to process, trying to figure us out. And, *Good,* I think. *Yes. Terror. Good.* Then it does, and the terror turns to something else. And *Jesus,* she whispers. *Sweet Jesus, is that you?* And she spins around, jumps up off the sofa, spreads her jiggly arms and shouts, O Halleluiah, Honeybear!

Come down, come down! My lamikimbs, my little dumplings have come home!

It just gets weirder and weirder by the second. Fucking freakshow. We've got the Bearded Lady, rubbing her eyes and blubbering about dumplings and honeybears. We've got the fat old fucker chugging down the stairs in make-up and a hot pink robe. Family reunion! The prodigals return! And for a second I think we'll all sit down for a nice big Christmas dinner.

Then Benjie chucks the crowbar at his head. That was a surprise—didn't see that coming. It misses, of course, sticks like a tomahawk in the wall behind him. Liberace squeals and takes off up the stairs. Beardo turns to us and shrieks, *Get thee behind me, Satan!* She jumps on Benjie's back, I jump on hers, we're spinning 'round the room, and Benjie breaks free and bolts up after him. And now it's just me and the grizzly—I'm trying to wrestle her down, but she's strong as hell and feisty and clawing at my face. Then we hear this loud *Bang!* and we stop. Then another sound like a *pop* and then a really big *KA-BOOM!* And we fall back on the carpet and everything gets real quiet.

Well, who could've known the fucker'd have a gun? I'm staring at the crowbar in the wall, it's like a crucifix. She's got her eyes pinned to the ceiling, listening. There's some movement, somebody shuffling around up there, real slow, then the sound of a footstep on the stairs. And she starts whimpering, Spiro? Honeybear, is that you? And shit if it is so I grab the bat and brain her. But it's Benjie who comes down around the corner. It's Benjie who comes down. And I see by the blood and the holes in his eyes it's fucked.

The gun misfired. (Of course it did.) Jammed on the second shot, blew up in his face on the third. Well, I'm just saying. He was lucky to have his head. But a whole lotta good that's gonna do us now. Brains, remember? *Brains are not enough.* Why the fuck'd you have to go and shoot him three times? I yell. And you know what he says? Here's proof of the brains. Standing there, blood streaming from his sockets, lining up the dominos. "Once is luck. Twice is coincidence—" *Twice is when the fucking luck runs out!* I scream. And now fuck if we're stuck with a body and a fucking truck no one can drive!

You'll drive, he says, in that voice I still remember in my dreams.

What the fuck do you mean I'll—

I'll show you, Carrie. You'll see. You'll be the eyes.

Meanwhile, back at the freak farm, Beardo's starting to twitch. What are we supposed to do with that? I ask.

We have to bring her, he says.

Are you fucking kidding me? Why don't we just shoot her, too?

And what do you think he says? (Predictably.) "You'll see."

And shit on it all if there's any arguing when he's got a notion in his head. So here we are—lugging out the guts, hauling them down the alley to the truck—the blind fucking leading the blind. Like literally. Well. There *had* been a plan. But God knows how we're ever going to get to it now.

But the funny thing is—the funny thing about it all, I swear— through all that shit, that cat, old Snowball, she didn't even blink. She just sat there, still as a statue, eyes like empty dice, smiling. Like she'd seen that shit-show coming—all of it—all along . . .

The plan *had* been to get to Canada. We were just three hours from the border. And—news flash—ready? We have a *shit-ton* of cash. Basically like our whole inheritance. Some trust fund, set up by our rich-ass Aunt Emma—because I guess like maybe she felt guilty all those years for not taking us herself. He'd gotten his hands on it just after juvie.

And every last cent of it, still untouched. He's just been trucking it around, stuffed in the berth, in that green Army duffle under Cassandra. *What the fuck, Benjie?* I said. I sure could've done with knowing that was laying around. He just grinned at me—or seemed to. We knew we'd find you someday, Carrie, he said.

But the main thing now is we've got to get the fuck out—get somewhere. *With* two bodies. And who knows what he's got cooking. But he's been driving these roads for years, remember? Up and down, back and forth—Carrie, he tells me, they're like the back of my hand. And I look and the back of his hand's all covered with blood. I just shake my head. But I get us in gear, get us back to the main road. And we're off. The night flight north. Winding up the invisible Finger Lakes, towards 90.

The night was very dark. He'd gone all silent. He had his head bowed in profile in the dashlight. For a second I thought he might be praying.

What's three? I asked. He raised his head.

What?

If one was luck and two's coincidence, what's three?

He looked over at me with those ruined holes of eyes and the jagged Joker smile that wasn't.

Three. Three is destiny, he said.

+

I was blind when I saw, cries Oedipus, as the awful truth of his life sweeps over. Misery will grind no man as it grinds you, the Chorus sings. Better never to have been born. Better not to have been conceived: the story that can only end, as it always ends, in misery. The pointless, boyish dream. There was no version of us that could ever be together. Not wholly so. Not one. But pointless? (*Only if you believe it's pointless now.*) Do you believe it to be? Be honest, Benjie.

She took my hand and put it on myself. It was starting to get hard. The tent was round and the dome curved over us and the light of the fire seen through it, a red pulsing skin. It's a magic wand, I said. You have to shake it.

Why can't I have a magic wand? she said.

They were talking outside in the firelight. Low, transparent voices.

It goes inside you and turns into a fish.

That's gross! she squealed.

"You children go to sleep."

She sat up and leaned and zipped the bag up over us. Dark and dark. In the first secret place.

Tomorrow we'll be seven.

Tomorrow we'll be born.

Night night, little fish.

Then we were one.

North. Route 96. Rounding the tip of Seneca to Geneva. 20 West to 5, where it splits, crossing the broad floodlights of 90 (beware the grizzly's claw). Entelechy. Be what the acorn knows. The oak unfurled, implicit in the seed. Branching of roads like limbs in air, adhering, presupposing. The seed. Follow the vital flow. A mother music. Listen for the mouth. Mmm. Mmm. Mmm. Mmm mm, mm, mm. (Repeat.) Mmm. Mmm. Mmm. Mmm mm, mm, mm. Sing the forgotten world into existence.

Her voice, low and watery in the minivan, in the black, the night washed over us. Their two forms in the front, gnomonesque, eclipsing

the lights of the dash. Cocooned in black, her music washing over us.
The tape on loop, all through the night, on the night road north, with

Mmm. Mmm. Mmm. Mmm mm, mm, mm.

(Repeat.)

Listen for the songline. The mouth—

Let us be lovers we'll marry our fortunes together

Sing the forgotten world— And, oh,

Time there was oh what a time there was it was

a time of innocence

The seed

*It was dawn when we finally arrived in Niagara. A pewter light, and a mist in
the trees, making the morning maples flare. Red squirrels running up to your
fingers to feed. And everywhere in the air, at the ear, like a high-off rushing of
wings, that sound. Come on, Carrie! I said.*

Don't go far, Mother called from the minivan.

*We ran across the greensward down to the rail where we could see it. Silver-
white, the mist invisibling the other side. White sinews like the necks of silver
horses hurtling forward. Far out, a spruce trunk, like the mast of a ship, shot up.
Oh my God, did you see that?*

*They were coming down the hill. Drowsy still, but easy in their bodies. He
was holding her hand, the wicker basket in the other. In the grainy light they
look like apparitions.*

You two take forever! I called.

*We walked along it to where the sidewalk rounded in a viewing station, a
semicircular outcropping jutting over. We stepped up, the four of us, to the rail.*

*Do you think they'll ever die? she asked. That was the falling. I closed
my eyes and fell like a darkness all the way down.*

Tonight we're six. In the morning we'll be seven.

They were talking still outside the tent. Low, easy, watery voices. The fire on the wall made it pulse like a rippling cave.

Do you think *we'll* ever die? she asked.

And the thrust so strong and the billowing so white a body could fall forever and never be found. A body could fall forever—

"Step back a little, children, from the rail," Father said.

So I knew if I could only get us to Niagara.

+

That's where we end. That's where it finishes. Our shit-show of a saga. In a firebomb—"Epic." As he used to say. But I just can't stop replaying it in my brain, wondering if it all really happened. If it really happened just *that* way. Because it had to have happened, right? I'm here, no one's denying that. But did it have to happen just that way?

Fucking avalanche. Fucking apocalypse.

Fucking Snowball.

I still see him, he comes to me, his boy face still washes up sometimes in a dream—at the edge of something—just the face, shaved clean, thin as an apple peel, without the body. He tells me things he has imagined for my life. Crazy things—things you wouldn't believe, not even if you read them in a story. I'm thirty-three (well, I *am* thirty-three—who would've believed she'd make it *this* long), I'm living in the City—that's not so unbelievable—but the crazy thing is, I'm in another body. Well. Same body, technically, I guess, same skin. The new hardware takes a little getting used to. But all that other—all of that that *was* ourselves, that whole fucked-up, miserable affair we agreed to call our life—wiped clean.

And the craziest thing of all he comes to tell me, from that place wherever it is the face drifts up then disappears, is that I, Carrie (no longer Carrie now, he calls me Cash), am happy. *Happy*. Imagine that. And free.

But like I said, we're not talking here of me.

It was about three in the morning when we finally got to Niagara. All dark, except for the weird yellow-green of the lights in the parking lot, and not a soul anywhere to be seen. It was that funny kind of feeling of being there before, but not exactly, the way the light had changed and you still had the memory of how it was, but now you're seeing everything like through this fish-light of a dream. Well. I did have the memory. We *had* been there before. Some family vacation when we were like five. That kind of memory, like being underwater. But for him, it was still all crisp and clean: he's going on about the trees and a grassy hill and misty light and squirrels coming up to your fingers to feed. And the sidewalk by the river leading down to a view of the Falls where he accidentally dropped a toy man over.

Of course, post 9/11, all that's changed. Good luck trying to get a tractor-trailer anywhere close. Freaking barriers and security checkpoint stations everywhere. But he's insisting, No, I'll tell you where to go, there's a *parking lot*—it's where we were—down by that little slope that drops down to the sidewalk by the river. And I'm like, Benjie. Dude. There's not even a road. And he's like, There is! There is! It's there, it runs along the river. And I'm like, excuse me, Dumbshit. Who's the one here with the eyes? I'm telling you, I can only get the truck this close.

Where are we now? he asks.

We're at some—I don't know—in front of some Information Center. He goes quiet for a second.

What Information Center?

What fucking Information—the one with fucking INFORMA-TION written on front, on that big-ass fucking sign hung up over the phones!

Hopeless to deal with when he has a notion in his head.

So anyway. I get the truck parked. And I'm like, all right, Einstein. Now what's the plan? And the plan is none fucking other than to throw the fat old fucker over the Falls. Which means of course we're gonna have to lug him. Fuck. It's like half a mile and he weighs more than a whale. *Why can't we just throw his fat ass over in the bushes?* But no, no, no, he's got a notion, he's going on about how he saw it—it was there, in the beginning, he saw it in the seed. The seed. See what I'm saying? This is what we're dealing with. He can't even see the fucking forest for—. Fuck it. He can't even see the trees.

So here we go, we pop the trailer latch, open the door. Beardo's sleeping peacefully (or so we think). Lug him out, carry him off. And predictably, the latch doesn't get reclosed.

We get back awhile later, the door's wide open.

Um. Benjie, I say. Beardo's gone.

What? he asks.

Looks like she helped herself to the door.

The door? How is that possible?

Well it doesn't take a genius to figure out—

You didn't reclose the latch? And I look at him like are you fucking kidding me—

Of course I didn't reclose the latch! Is it my fucking truck? I thought *you* were on it!

And he's just blank-faced staring. But I can see the wheels inside, grinding, trying to figure something out. It's not that complicated, Benj, the door was open and she opened it—

She opened the door, he says. And it's more like something he's remembering than saying. His voice is weird—it's got that singsong-mechanical ring—and his eyeless eyes—it's starting to freak me out. She opened the door . . . She opened the door—just that, over and over. Then he rears back, gives this loud half-laugh, half-wail to the sky and he's hammering his eyes, hollering like some freaking retard—*Oh God! How could I not see it?* "She opened the door!"

She fucking opened it! I scream. *Somebody didn't fucking shut it!* And if *you* don't fucking shut it now and pull yourself together, we are seriously very seriously *fucked!*

He looks at me. Or—you know—looks in my direction, with that carved-out Joker smile that wasn't.

Oh Carrie, he says, very cool, very calm. Very fucked is all we ever were to be.

What are you talking about? I ask.

The door, he says. She opened it. She was the ticket.

The ticket what? Ticket where? And it's almost, I don't know, pity—a helpless, heartsick broken pity that I see ripple across his ruined eyes.

With her, he says, they would have had to let us over.

So she was the ticket. But of course by now the ticket's waddled off halfway to Hoboken. I spend awhile swatting around in the bushes with the bat trying to find her. Finally we just give up. In that time she's gotten herself to a phone, called the cops, given them the whole story, our APB, GPS, whatever, and they're waiting for us—we're shark bait—just up the road.

The way that final shit went down . . . And this is the part I'm always replaying, always trying to re-remember another way. Like what if I'd tricked him into getting down first out of the cab? Then we both might have made it. We both might have gotten away clean. But then

I see it's no use trying to change it. There was never any other way it could have been. There was no other way it would have possibly gone down. Because why? He had a notion.

We'd driven up the backroads to the bridge a few miles north, the one with a big state park beside it. And as we turned into the highway and came around the bend, I'm like *Holy fucking Christ*. You wouldn't believe the size of that trap. Tell me, he said. It's like fucking Coney Island, freaking roller coasters, Ferris wheels. All lit up, it's like the bridge is on fire and the whole sky blazing.

Where?

Straight in front of us! Straight ahead! Benjie, I tell him, I'm scared.

How far? he asks.

I dunno, maybe a hundred yards? I was never good at directions. Close enough to see them scrambling. They see us.

Cut the lights, he says. Get down out of the cab. He reaches back in the berth and yanks up the Army duffle and tosses it down to me on the ground. *Now, Carrie, run!* What? Where the fuck—? Run where? *Just run!* he screams and slams the door and hammers the knob lock down. And I'm looking around and there's nothing behind me but woods and dark. And the sirens and whirling lights are starting to stream down. They're coming. And I think for a second, Shit, is this really it? Is he really just going to go and leave me again? Then I see it. Holy fuck do I see it. I see what he's got planned.

He reaches back in the berth, grabs Cassandra, hauls her up, fastens her into the seat by his side. And I jump up and I'm banging on the door trying to open it calling his name but he won't hear me. And that's the memory: the two of them—her, blank-eyed and smiling, wearing his green trapper's hat where he's shoved it onto her head; him, his long, greasy hair and holes for eyes, jaw clenched, the dark scar wiggling. Like a worm, I think, struggling under the skin. That's how I see him. Now. For always. And he turns to me and mouths something in the glass. What was it? What were those words, I wonder?

He throws the truck into gear, hits the headlights, grips the wheel. The big rig surges forward towards the bridge. I hang on while I can, till the sirens and flashes fuse to white and I fall back as it all goes under.

+

In that world I have imagined for us, that inward space where memory and lost potential play, where there's no longer any pain, and the names are changed, and we have no need of these old bodies, I find her again from my distance, in the pixel screen, and she remembers me like a face that she once wore—maybe in a dream—before she steps into her new life like a set of freshly purchased clothes, or a newly fashioned body.

It's New York City, after all, where a person can be anyone.

And it gives me pleasure thinking if she is, she is a man.

It comforts me.

It lets me see the dream of one.

BE STILL MY SOUL

If there is one verse I have claimed in my life more often than any other, it is this: *Whom the Lord loves, He chastiseth.* There is such comfort in that. There is such comfort in knowing all of our burdens and trials are evidence of His deep and abiding compassion. That He corrects us like a loving father out of the brambles of error, onto the path of light and truth. For truly, all of us, like sheep, have gone astray, as Scripture teaches. But remember also: He leadeth me; His rod and His staff, they comfort me. The faithfulness of His Word abideth forever. Praise Him.

But the children.

It is not always easy to discern His compassionate hand when you look at the children. Such pain they've suffered. Such burdens they have, some of them, had to bear. Just unspeakable, some of the things I've seen. I tell you, the Prince of Darkness is alive and well and at work on this planet, you have only to look at the children to see that. In the lives of the poor defenseless. In the adults responsible. Whom they, the innocent, too often grow up to become. An eye for an eye, as Scripture warns. We are called as His ambassadors to be vigilant.

But of the thirty-seven children we have fostered in our time, they were the greatest trial, the greatest burden. And she and her brother, they were the ones with the advantages! The material ones, I mean. Well-off parents who provided and protected. I took it upon myself, as I have done with each of our children, to provide the spiritual manna, the scriptural meat. The fear of the Lord and the yielding to His teachings. I have seen Him work wonders in the hearts of the broken young. I still receive letters, from all over the globe, testifying to His ongoing work in their lives.

I believe that each of us has a particular duty that God has laid out for us. The children have been mine. I believe that each of our lives has a plan, a beautiful purpose, whether or not it is given to us to clearly discern it. And it is a beautiful thing, truly beautiful, when by the aligning of our wills with His, we are allowed the grace to achieve it.

That's certainly what I've thought with each of our children. I remember thinking it very clearly, very distinctly, with them, those two, when they came to us, after the tragic death of their parents. Providential, it seemed: the way it happened in our very town, and we just happening to have an empty house, I had made fresh application and was waiting. I remember praying, Lord, if it be Thy will, allow those lambs to come to us. It would be such a blessing for them not to have to be carried away. Let them remain together. Let them come to us. I can give them a sense of Your purpose and plan, O Lord, if it be Thy will. Suffer those little ones to come unto me.

Of course now I have to wonder. Now I have to pause. I remember I must not lean on my own understanding. Sometimes God brings mystery into our lives, not to break us, but to make us broader. To extend our souls into a greater union with His. Who is all light. But we are engaged in a great spiritual battle, spiritual warfare, with a powerful enemy: the Father of Lies. The Prince of Appearances and Author of Deceit. Sometimes we can be blinded by what only appears to be the light; at other times it is by darkness we most clearly see. There are some deceptions even the angels cannot detect. To truly tell the darkness from the light: this may be the deepest mystery, the deepest form of grace.

They taught me that. And for it, I am grateful. Though I must confess, at times I nearly thought it would kill me. I thought sometimes they were quite literally trying to kill me. Oh, it was hardly anything as blatant as open war; we know from Scripture that is seldom how the Enemy operates. He preys on us through indirection and suggestion; is subtle-potent, uses wiles and delicious guile, touching us where we feel ourselves the strongest. How they made me believe for a time that they were mine; that at last I had found in these lambs the two who would love and cherish me as much as I had so, in the beginning, wanted to love and cherish them. The way they would bound to my open arms, their hunger for spiritual nourishment, their attentiveness and quiet, they were so quiet—the pictures of innocence and compliance. And beauty, you had never seen in their whiteness and radiance on Earth two more angelic forms. I counseled them continually on the perils of that burden, warned them of the snares of vanity and self-love, admonished them how, with such a gift, much is expected in return. And they looked at me then with all the adoration deserved by our first mother, Eve.

Indeed, when I look back on those days, I see cast over them the hazy morning light of Eden, the glow in the Garden when the Man and the Woman walked and communed with their Maker. I see myself, moving among the duties of the house, attended by two almost spirits. In my joy (for it was that) I imagined their faces somehow not their own, but lit from within by a fire that I had kindled, that drove away the shadows of the past, and made us one.

What I would have given only to remain indefinitely in that dream.

One night I was awakened by calls, loud cries, coming from their bedroom. I rose and hurried down the hall, removing the keys from around my neck (I never was without them), hastening to their door and quickly opening the lock. Bright moonlight and frigid autumn

air streamed in from the open window—it occurred to me to repri-
mand them for such heedlessness—falling onto his little bed where
they both were huddled. Ghost-white, shivering in each other's arms,
they seemed not to be aware of my entrance, even when I walked to
the window and pulled it closed, pulled the curtain back over the bars
and turned on the overhead light; they continued to stare at the patch
on the bedspread where the beam of light had fallen. I saw that her
fingertips were rosy with fresh blood where she had chewed them.
What is it, children? I asked. Lambs? There was no reply, only a deep
and wordless shudder as he rolled over and buried his face in his sister's
arms. She looked at me then. Her eyes, very calm, seemed not entirely
to see me and her voice when she spoke was deeper, older. I do not
think they will be coming back tonight, she said. Who? I asked. She
turned her eyes to the window. I felt the blood rising into my temples
at the thought of some stranger, some intruder, in the house, but that
fear was immediately dispelled by the bars and the lock safeguarding
the door. Someone was outside? I pressed. Tell me! I went to her and
shook her. But she turned without another word to her brother, laying
her head over his still shivering form. I was about to dismiss the whole
episode as mere imagination, a childish game, when something caught
my eye on the floor between the window and the bed. It was a saw, a
handsaw, with a thin gray blade, the kind used by my husband to cut
pool piping. What are you doing with this? I asked. The boy looked up.
They brought it, he said with frightened eyes. My blood was beginning to boil with impatience. The prank had run its course; it was late,
the middle of the night, and I was angry and confused about the saw.
Clearly, they had been rifling through things not theirs. But when? And
what else had they taken?

Back to sleep, I told them. I folded them in and locked the door,
intending to have a full account in the morning.

But at breakfast they insisted. They refused to be shaken from their story that they had *seen* something, some presence, at the window, that had motioned for them to open it and had dropped the handsaw in. I resolved to end the mystery then and there, taking them with the item out to the shed where my husband kept his tools. But a paralyzing thought struck me as we crossed the yard and came to the door: How had they gotten past *that* lock? Not only the question of when in the day they had had occasion—for, beside their daily quiet times in their room, they were constantly by my side—but how and from where they had secured the key. One hung at my neck; the other was kept in my husband's bureau, and any thought of the two of them discovering a way into our bedroom, rummaging through our items, incensed me to no end. I sent them back to their room to begin their morning lessons and decided to end the mystery of the saw myself. But something happened just then that filled me with more profound and ponderous wonder.

I had turned with them back towards the house and was watching them make their way across the lawn. My heart was cloudy with a newly felt sensation of trouble and distrust. They had never before this given me any indication of disloyalty; they had always presented their love and devotion as truly open-faced and transparent. But now they were hiding something from me: not only was it the matter of the theft—though the item itself was less important to my mind than the fact that they'd conspired somehow against me to procure it—and then had lied about its coming to them, by way of a fanciful invention. And furthermore (and this certainly contributed to my agitated state), the momentary fear of an intruder in the house had so disrupted my sense of security and peace—even though it had been quickly dispelled as an impossible suspicion—that I hadn't been able to sleep. My mind was restless; as I lay in bed, it had combed mysteriously back through the years, as if carried by a will other than my own. Faces of children and moments long forgotten had surfaced and amazed me with their apple crispness. It had seemed to me, before this, in hazy retrospect, that these two beautiful creatures had been the crown—a culminating gift merely pre-shadowed by that long line of disfigured, unfortunate others; but now, under the power of these vivid impressions, I felt each face that arose evoke in me its own individual aura of affection and the love, the fierce, undeniable love I had had for them, each blessed miracle of them, each in its own brief time.

Still in these thoughts, watching them go into the house, I became aware of other eyes watching mine. There was a window overlooking the back yard, on the second story just above the kitchen, that belonged to a kind of hutch I had used in earlier years, once when the house-hold had swelled past seven children. I'd built a scrim to form a little room; it hadn't been inhabited since that time and had now become an overflow for storage and supplies. Four sisters from Romania had slept there.

I don't know by what hand of Providence it was that in that instant my eyes were directed towards that upstairs window. But as I looked, I felt my body seize with terror. Two figures, a man and a woman, stood framed together in the glass, motionless, surveying the scene below them on the lawn. In my stupor, in my bewilderment of shock and disbelief, I fumbled to focus, gradually taking them in. He was tall, with rich, dark hair; hers as well, her head rising to his shoulder, with two long, thin needles or wands gathering it in back, making her seem Oriental. They were dressed entirely in black, which gave them an air of severity and formality. But their faces, hideously twisted and gaunt, suggested deprivation and hunger in the extreme: indeed, the longer I stared they seemed to be almost skinless, skeletal. And the *expression* there—his lip's contemptuous curl; her own, frozen into an arrogant sneer; and the hate in their eyes as they glared at me—at *me*—as with some sinister intent, some dreadful, yet-unspoken accusation—.

But the children! They had entered the house and were by now, I imagined, moving through the kitchen just below, on their way back to their room. As if sensing their progress, the two in the window had stepped back from my view. It would be just a quick walk down the stairs for them to intercept them, and then—. My mind broke off at that unthinkable possibility. I had to move quickly. Without question, there was some evil in the house, an intruder more terrible than any I had imagined the night before. My heart was still frozen from that look of horrible purpose, almost vengeance, on their faces.

When I reached their room, I found the door swung open and the two of them there, sitting at their desks, quietly at work on their lessons. There was no sign anywhere of the others—not on the stairs, in the kitchen, not the hall or back utility, not in my bedroom. There was still the upstairs to search, but I was too terrified to let them out of my sight. And to take them with me while I scoured the house—no, nothing seemed to me of greater importance in that moment than to keep them innocent of the danger. These two, I reasoned, must have been "they" who had appeared at their window the night before, the two that had so frightened them. I couldn't be sure what in the darkness they had seen. But one thing was certain: the threat had entered the house. I felt paralyzed with that knowledge. I couldn't leave their side, couldn't call anyone for help. To tell, to admit such a terrible breach, what would that be but to risk losing them?

As I sat on the bed, in my exhausted state, in that trembling numbness and blankness of mind that had followed in the aftermath of the encounter, I became aware, again, of my vision being filled by that series of faces from the night before, the souls I had tended over the years. In my distress I thought—and my poor heart warmed at this—that they had come, all of them now, to minister to me. *It's all right. It's all right*, they seemed to say, each in its own sweet way, with its own little individual lisps and liltings. Oh, they had been so broken. And it had been my aim, my duty, indeed I had devoted all I was, my *all-in-all*, to protect them, to provide for them a safe, healing haven. To show them a sense of His unfolding purpose and plan. I still received letters, from all over the globe, testifying to the ongoing work of His presence in their lives.

My two lambs, as if sensing this, rose from their desks and came and nestled in my arms. What is it, Mama? they meekly asked. Such innocence almost broke my heart. I gathered them close and wept quiet tears; I prayed, prayed fervently, as I have always done, for a hedge of protection to be planted around our house, against the Evil One. I knew in that moment, with the faces of my flock, all of them, swimming in my eyes, and the two of them held so closely at my breast, more deeply and more certainly than I had ever known, the depth and the power and glory of that word: *Mother*. There was no other on this Earth. It was given to me to defend them alone.

Later that night, after they had gone to sleep, I satisfied myself that the upstairs also was empty. There was no reason to open every door—the padlocks remained in place; the two, whoever they were, had obviously exited the house downstairs through the front entrance as they saw me advancing from the shed across the yard. Still, something compelled me—nostalgia perhaps; sweet memories of an earlier, blessed time—to reenter those rooms and stand there in the dark, in the bars of moonlight falling across the floor, communing with those spirits of the past, whom my constant care and nourishment had molded. I imagined them now as grown, moving freely through the world, fraught with care and responsibility; some of them, I knew from their letters, had small children of their own. They had taken on the burden, healing the hearts of the broken young, becoming missionaries and ambassadors. I felt so proud, but also lonely. I had given so much of myself, over the years it felt like so much of myself had simply flown away.

But how good it had been, how green, back then, just to bask in nothing more than the beauty of another day. The frolicking sun and apple blossom, the dew still on the roses. All the laughter and love that a houseful of children could bring. I could see on the floors where their little beds had lain, the marks on the doors made by their precious hands. I could almost hear their voices, still stirring in the walls, like a nest of baby squirrels at sleepy play.

I had walked to the window and was leaning against it, musing out through the bars at the moonlight on the lawn. In the shade of the sycamore where we all had sat I could see, huddled together, dark forms—a trick of the eyes, I thought, from the broken light falling on the scattered clumps of autumn leaves. As I looked, they sleepily rocked, some of them, to and fro in the breeze; one raised its head as if to stretch then nestled back into its bed of leaves. Not leaves, I suddenly saw as two walked forward into the wavering light, but geese—a flock of passing geese had landed on our lawn. My heart welled up with tears and welcome; it truly seemed a miracle and a sign. They had come, these nighttime travelers, these spirit ministers, on this night above all, as if summoned. (As if something in *me* summoned, something called.) Oh nothing, I saw, not the least of us, not even the last, was lost. We were, all of us, being gathered. Heaven had spread its hands against the sky.

Warmed by that vision, I looked in on them before retiring to the downstairs sofa, where I intended to sleep in order to be more quickly available should anything arise. They were sleeping peacefully in their beds; all was in its place; the window had been securely fastened with a vise. But I couldn't rest. I kept thinking about the saw. Like some insidious mist it hovered. The distrust it had engendered had been temporarily dispelled by the sudden threat of danger in the house, but now it returned to haunt the edges of my mind, and drifted gradually to the center. They had claimed that something, someone, had dropped it into the room. Was that possible? Perhaps. But only *after* the intruder had procured it from the shed, and the lock proved that impossible. Unless ... Had they somehow conspired with the mysterious guests? That really was unthinkable. To picture any intercourse between such innocence and—*those two* ... and then, again, when would they have had occasion? I recalled with some surprise that I still hadn't settled the matter: had the tool even come from the shed? I resolved before speculating any farther to put that lingering question to rest.

I rose from the sofa and crept quietly to the kitchen and opened the pantry where I had locked it away secretly. But among the piles of old picnic baskets and scrapbooks stacked inside, it wasn't there. I distinctly remembered—but perhaps I had stored it in one of the cabinets. Or the drawers. It wasn't anywhere. I thought for a moment I must be losing my mind; I even went so far as to open the oven and the refrigerator. All the locks were intact. I alone possessed the keys. I had hidden it here, I could almost swear I had. But where?

The thought came to me that maybe *they* had hidden it. I even thought for an instant they might have it in one of their beds, under their pillow, just to torment me, knowing I'd never suspect it. It was impossible. And yet my head was full of such wild imaginings. Well, the thing certainly hadn't flown off all by itself! I resolved to return to the question of the shed, my mind darkening with unease and suggestion.

I stepped out the back door and moved quickly over the lawn. The geese were gone, and the moon had disappeared beneath a low line of rapidly gathering clouds. Still, the desolation fortified me. I felt the hand of Heaven at my back, and the thought of remembered manna at my feet swelled in my heart as I neared the darkened structure. But something was wrong, I saw, as I stepped closer. In the shadows, an angle was off. The door—it was ajar. The lock hung gaping in its slide. How was that possible? With a chill I turned and felt my eyes again directed to the upstairs window. It was dark, but still in the glass I could see them lingering, like some insidious dream, some dark, unthinkable suggestion. The hate was still there, and along with it a look of trium- phant mockery as they sneered down on my confusion. O God, who were they at all? Why would they want to hurt us? When I had given all, I had given all—. At the word, those shadowy others, as if sum- moned to my defense, came rushing forward—all my ministering an- gels—battering the upstairs glass as if to scatter, force down those hid- eous faces. I saw them again as through a lighted scrim, all the broken years of them, the mutilated, maimed, all my helpless darlings, flocking to my aid. And still, such hunger at the lips, my babes, lips lapping for a drop of Mother's milk, white manna from my breast, a crumb, the littlest crust, *please, please,* they seemed to lisp—. The vision faded. The upstairs hutch was dark. But I knew my heart twice-fortified. If not for me, then it must be for my defenseless little ones. My soul was steeled, my spirit girded, as for war.

I opened the door of the shed. I knew full well there was an evil here outside my apprehension. I could sense it in the clouds louring above the house, could smell it like the tincture of chlorine in my dreams. It was gathering, I could hear it, in the midnight of the shed, licking and unfolding its great wings . . .

There they were, in a line in the shadows, the tools, hanging on the pegs—orderly as children awaiting my inspection. As after bath, how inno- cent, how innocuous they would seem. How I had so wanted to believe them mine. And yet how prone, susceptible to darker purposes, beneath the Enemy's hand . . . My heart, I felt it could explode. If the saw was gone, they clearly had betrayed me. (If it was here, had I betrayed my-self with meaningless suspicion? And yet I'd *seen* it, I had hidden it!) The walls were beginning to swim. I hadn't slept; I had, I had kept vigilant. Through all the years of them. Still. My soul knew some de-ceptions even the angels couldn't detect. Through the gloom, I moved to them again and reached as if into the wound where the instrument had hung—and where it *was* (my vision closed and opened): the very make and shape, the seeming shadow of the same I saw now in my hand—*my* hand that drifted with horror and bewilderment to my face. As if *I* had dropped it in . . . Impossible! I shook it violently away. And as the phantom fell and disappeared, and the shadows on the wall also dissolved, as the shed itself in shadow seemed to quiver and congeal, I heard behind me the unmistakable clicking shut of a door and the low, gradual sliding of the lock.

O lambs. Forgive me. He really had me now. O children. I was really in the dark.

Heaven alone can tell what torments I endured that night. Vision after vision: the house lit up, the upstairs rooms ablaze. Figure after figure in the halls, along the walls—the doors flung open, all the locks agape: emaciated forms, they mouth at me and lunge, lips livid with unutter-able rage. I call their names, I see the scattered ones, all the lost sons and daughters of this house; I gather them in my arms, they come undone, just unintelligible sounds, no longer human names—

> *Rodica. Edwina.*
> *Ananth. Ioanela.*
> *Ekaterina. Cosmina.*
> *Xiaoli . . .*

And *they* are there, they meet me on the stairs, grown now and savage from wandering on the Earth. In all the truth time would in all its radiance reveal: Godless eyes, their blossom of beauty wasted, ghastly white, the obscene flowers of leprosy. Gaunt as the crowbar hanging from his hand. Her face, an open nest of scabs. Just a scrap, a smudge of what once turned the world's blind head. A Jezebel not even the dogs would touch.

(But I have prayed a hedge about this house. He has made the weapon of mine enemy to explode in fatal fury about his face. He has hounded my adversary into outer dark, the keys to a flaming chariot in her hand—)

Eighteen gears, the policemen told us after. Where on Earth did she think she was going in that truck?

All falls to dark. The upstairs rooms again are quiet. And in mute wonder shall I spend the remainder of my days. His Word have I locked with His mystery in my heart. How inscrutable His justice; how vast, outside all understanding, His ways.

WADE IN THE WATER

Spiro Zyklos was the unlikely name of the man bent over the pool pump, struggling to unclog it from the flip-flop strap that had inexplicably drifted in. A flip-flop strap, he puzzled. Why would a flip-flop strap be floating unattached? And (reaching his fingers deep into the mechanism's throat) what had happened to the sole?—just at that moment seeing the Boxer watching him from inside the living room window, a woman's pink thong dangling from its jowls. *Bingo* . . . Spiro had solved some pretty mysterious clogs in his day. Some didn't require a degree in rocket science. Condoms and pizza crusts, maybe some wing bones thrown in: pool party, the parents out of town. Sometimes, though, it took a little putting together. There was the case of the self-propelled Roaming Shark™. When he unscrewed the lid of the shuddering object, he was met with a gigantic wad of semen and pubic hair. *Hm* . . . He turned the gadget over in his latex glove. He'd not seen this model before. At a twitch in the bushes he glanced up, just in time to catch the teenaged boy slinking guiltily away. He turned his eyes to the vacuum again: at the center of its underbelly, a perfectly sized, still straining, slurping hole . . .

In his twenty-five years as a pool cleaner and repairman, really Spiro had seen it all. Couples fucking on loveseats with the blinds drawn up, young housewives at kitchen windows in their bras. Or not. He'd seen some pretty considerable breasts in his time. He tried not to think about them too hard. They only reminded him of the conquests of his youth and how now, pressing sixty, all that was probably behind him. Plus there was Gladys, his wife. He sighed. *Ah, niata. Perasmena megalea.* Everything passes. He'd give it a few more years till he retired. He could do that whenever he wanted, it was his business. And then? He looked up. The sun was high, a platinum disc over the cloudy Ithaca suburb. They should really do something nice. Maybe he'd take her on a cruise, to the Aegean Islands; they'd not been back there since their honeymoon. But it'd have to be soon, if she was going to remember it, that was. Her mind was beginning to get a little hazy.

But it always amused him, honestly it almost made him laugh, to think of all those people he'd seen. It was as if, sometimes, they had *intended* him to see them. As if they'd wanted to be seen. On the one hand, it was innocuous enough: he was the pool man, just your average, anonymous Joe. He kept at a distance; he certainly wasn't a threat. He'd never be intimately involved. People had their fetishes, their little fantasies, he knew that. Whole drawers-full of kinky little whatnots and supplies. If they needed an outside party to get the fluids pumping, he could provide that. At no extra charge. He'd perform his services and leave without a word. Swing back next week to see how things were getting on. He could be that. The Keeper of the Secret. The detached, yet ever-necessary, Eye.

In his younger years, Spiro had worked as a professional wrestler on the New York/New Jersey circuit, never attracting the crowds of a "Gorgeous George" Wagner or Jimmy Londos, "The Golden Greek"—and never securing the much-hoped-for television contract—but acquiring considerable notoriety as a stage name all the same. Spiro "The Human Spear" thrilled audiences with his signature in-ring flight, rebounding off the ropes and propelling himself into the solar plexus of his opponents. A fatal blow, it never failed. When after the bell he rose

over the body of his rival—and some of them were among the bright-
est names of the day in this, what still was known as wrestling's first
Golden Age—hired nymphs in skimpy Hellenic garb tossed rose petals
into the ring as Spiro strutted godlike beneath the crowd's abounding
cheers and the loudspeakers pumping the Greek national anthem.

The rose gimmick he'd cribbed from Gorgeous George. From the
time he was seven, when the then still ascending star made his debut on
national television, Spiro had been fascinated—obsessed even—with
the flamboyant personality: his effeminate platinum curls and resplen-
dent silken robes; the red carpet rolled out before him by Jefferies,
his valet, who showered his master with rose petals and, with clouds
of Chanel No. 5, ceremoniously anointed the ring. If George Wagner,
a nobody from Butte, Nebraska, could make it in this business, anyone could. And he wasn't even that accomplished as a wrestler! It was
all glamor—"gorgeous" hype. From pork-and-beans poverty he had
climbed to become the highest paid professional athlete in the world—
friends with Bob Hope and Lucille Ball!—one of the most famous
celebrities of his time. He had done it, George Wagner, he had reached
for and seized the platinum star. He had dared to assume the audacious,
gorgeous dream.

Spiro still recalled standing outside Madison Square Garden that
drizzly February evening in 1949, a new nine-year-old just four years
in the country. His father was standing shivering beside, in his best wool
suit, holding $1.25—the change from the bag of street popcorn he'd
bought them after finding the fifty-cent balcony seats sold out. How
something inside the boy changed that evening, listening to the crowd
inside, the thunderous applause and waves of chanting and laughter
and jeers. He could almost see George, the featured attraction, strutting
to the ring amid showers of petals, Jefferies unpinning and folding the
silken robe before ascending with the perfume; he could hear George's

signature cry of mock-outrage, "Get your filthy hands off of me!" as the referee went to search his tights. But most of all, he could envision the gleam of the platinum-dyed curls under the high ring lights: how they shone like a discus in the rich billowing clouds of tobacco smoke. He would see that hair in his dreams. He would see, just ten years on, its humiliating end at the hands of Whipper Billy Watson: sitting with tears streaming down, staring at the screen as, live from Toronto's Maple Leaf Gardens, before 20,000 fans and over a million viewers, Whipper Billy planted his knee on the fallen hero's neck and lowered the Remington electric razor into those gorgeous, gorgeous locks . . .

By that time, 1959, Spiro had been in training for four years. Every day, before and after school—and even during, when he could get away with it—he was building his bulk and refining his technique at the YMCA in Queens. Under a trainer, he had mastered traditional Greco-Roman grappling and had moved on to the more popular American, pioneer-days tricks of "Catch-as-Catch-Can." He saw the future: how everything was changing, swelling, conglomerating—new national alliances replacing the regional companies of the past. With TV, the sport was becoming a network industry, the potential for audiences previously unforeseen—a great, faceless, amorphous primetime entity hungry for spectacle, acrobatics, something "extreme." Gone were the days of the traveling carnivals, of Polish and Czech yokels under a makeshift tarp rolling up their sleeves. Even wrestling itself seemed, to a degree, a thing of the past. Muscle and moves were still the tools of the trade, of course, but also, increasingly, masks. It would be just three years until the great coup de théâtre in Los Angeles' Olympic Auditorium, with Gorgeous George faced-off against "The Destroyer" in a final showdown of "Mask vs. Hair." Mask would prevail; George would again be shorn, in the next year would be dead. Young Spiro saw his silver star ascending with the bowing of that gorgeous, vanquished head.

He'd met Gladys in the summer of 1957. A department store clerk, two years his senior, she'd come down from Yonkers to attend the Billy Graham Crusade before leaving for Illinois in September to enter Wheaton College. The New York City Crusade had been extended to sixteen weeks; she'd signed on as a volunteer during its final month in August, handing out tracts and New Testaments on street corners in the vicinity of Madison Square Garden. It was a dream come true for the young woman—the opportunity of a lifetime—to do the Lord's work in the City during the days and sit each evening among the thousands who had come, and were coming still, to hear the dashing young evangelist— elegant and eloquent—whom the newspapers had dubbed "God's Heartthrob." The fact that he was an alumnus of her future alma mater only contributed to the aura of Providence.

She had taken a guest room, along with two other young women also helping with the Crusade, out in Queens, at the YMCA. Afford- able lodging, modest but clean, just a short train ride away from the Garden; and there were hours restricted in the morning for women who wanted to use the pool. That would be nice, she thought: before heading out to pound the August pavement of Manhattan, she could float, belly-up, and reflect upon the mystery of her young life that was now really beginning to open. There was a palpable sense of purpose in her being here, she thought; nothing was random—as the colored woman had sung last night before Mr. Graham arose, *For His eye is on the sparrow . . . And I know He watches me.* As she floated in the water, re- calling the singer's voice, its luscious dark and earthy contralto, and the sureness with which she had enunciated those lines, Gladys seemed to see, hovering above her, the Brylcreemed hair and chiseled cheekbones of the evangelist, nodding at her reassuringly. It was true: His eye *was* on us; if God could see the sparrow's fall, if He has the hairs of our heads, each of them, numbered, we know that He watches us, that He loves us, that He cares for us, and we know from His Word that He loves us so much that He sent His only begotten Son to die that we might have life hereafter. Do you *know* that you are a Christian? That had been the message of the sermon the night before: Are you living the Christ-filled life? Does your life bear witness to the fruits of the spirit? And if you died tonight, O sinner, ask yourself in your heart-of-hearts, with fear and earnest trembling, do you know—do you *know*—where you would spend eternity?

Gladys knew. And it pained her to no end to think of the thousands of lost souls who had never found, and might possibly never find, the joy of the Lord in their lives—the joy of knowing, with absolute and unshakable certainty, the loving hand of the Father upon them—

She glanced at the large clock hanging over the entrance to the pool. It was time. Through the fogged glass, she could see the young men lining up, eager to make their entrance. Modestly covering herself with a towel, she made her way to the side locker room, showered and put on her robe and took the back stairwell up to her room. Today it was going to be a scorcher, the weatherman had predicted. She dressed in her white silk sleeveless blouse, with the navy-blue polka-dotted skirt and hat; fastened the "Ambassador for Christ" pin smartly to her collar; took her New Testaments and box of tracts and walked downstairs.

He was coming around the corner of the building, from the weight-room showers, in a blind rush for school. They collided in a flash as her box burst open and the pea-green tracts sailed skyward, a pile of New Testaments clutched frantically between her hands. She sat there on the pavement, stunned for a moment, as he mumbled confused apologizes and blushed, scrambling to retrieve the scattered brochures with their boldfaced question, WHERE WILL *YOU* SPEND ETERNITY? from among the moving bodies of the rush-hour crosswalk. At last, he came and helped her to her feet. After all these years, she still remembered his words as he handed her back the stack of green tracts: "Gee, I'd like to spend eternity with *you.*" It was brash, as she later related to her girlfriends. But now, looking back, was it not also true? Didn't the whole thing (if one believed in such a thing) seem predestined? Hadn't it all been foreseen?

She invited him to the Crusade that evening. He met her there, at the entrance to the Garden, a little awed and full of memories of the last time eight years ago he had stood in that sidewalk's very square, through a disastrous birthday's February drizzle. But now, he thought, how different. As he watched the crowds of people filing in, smartly dressed and decent, and the two of them among them—the *two* of them!—he, Spiro, seventeen, with this very attractive Gladys at his side, confident and full of purpose (how she led him by the elbow down the aisle to his seat and smiled and told him over and over again how happy she was he'd come)—and the stage, so huge, and the choir made up of thousands, and the thousands upon thousands who'd also come . . . He could almost hear—in the echoes of their milling before the great and profound hush as the featured speaker was ushered in, and the organ opened its low and reverential tones—that crowd that as a boy had filled his ears, but from the outside listening in, as the Hero, still ascending, took the ring in a shower of unseen petals like the falling away of years, the melting away of droplets of platinum snow . . . The gorgeous moment. It had come. And here he was.

He bowed his head that night at the evangelist's bidding, and when called to the front, he came, with the hundreds of others, to stand at the foot of the makeshift cross and receive Christ as his personal Lord and Savior. As the organ played softly and the choir swooningly sang "Just as I Am," he rose from his seat, as the sermon had said, to become a new creature, to become a new man, for it seemed to him the old was passing away; behold, all things had become new. The voice of the evangelist had called him that night into a life filled with purpose, with direction, certainty—a life made strong by daily discipline and denial, by the curbing of his will to the will of the Father—and he rose with Gladys next to him, hand-in-hand, and moved forward. Her tears for him were tears of joy; her hand on his shoulder as he bowed his head and invited Christ into his life was a lily, or an orchid, some infinitely pure and delicate thing, and her body shook in little gasps and spasms as the two of them knelt together at the front and prayed. After it was over, they walked for a long time in silence up through Rockefeller Center. The heat of the day had lifted, and in the calm meanderings of a breeze the streets felt mysteriously, stirringly alive—all awash, atingle with an inkling they both had, but hadn't yet spoken, not yet, of unseen paths and passages opening before them, in this place and in the heart: heady plans and aspirations, all the unknown still to come, kept for them, and unmistakably beneficent, like light stored up in future suns. To be young in the City; to be two young people stepping together through its night, among all the millions who have made their anonymous way, somewhere, to someone . . .

When they came to the Y in Queens they parted. It was the first of many evenings that would end that way, meeting at the Crusade, walking and talking after, growing closer. He told her of his life—how he, the oldest now of seven children, had been called on to provide after his father's streetcar injury, his father the smalltime deli-owner who ridiculed his son's conversion. His older brother, Elias, who'd contracted polio four years ago this summer and had died. The incessant prayers of his mother for the boy, for Spiro, now, and the perils of his soul. For what was worse in her mind than being Protestant? (Well, Roman Catholic: Hadn't God prepared in Hell a special Pope-shaped hole?) One morning while shaving he'd discovered a small cross fingered surreptitiously in soot behind his left ear. He recognized that sign, he knew whose magnetic, mascaraed Evil Eye that Old-World talisman was for.

In September, she was gone. Letters followed, with further unburdening. Further encouragement, further emboldening. You must count it all joy, she wrote to him, knowing this: that the testing of your faith builds perseverance. Who takes up his cross and follows me, said Christ, must be prepared to forsake all others. Mother and father, sister and brother. Keep your eyes on the prize, my Spiro. Fight the good fight. And fight he had: that year he worked harder than ever, disciplining his body, building up its bulk, beating his will into submission. We are warriors in this world, she'd written. Boxers, *wrestlers*, says the Apostle; we are bearers of the light. Each opponent that he matched himself against he saw as a spiritual sign—the physical embodiment of a cosmic struggle against the forces of darkness and night. He would be *God's* Warrior, she told him when she visited at Christmas. They were standing in Times Square at the turning of the year. In the legions of our Lord, he would be the Savior's Spear.

It had a good ring to it, he thought. "The Savior's Spear." He'd have to explore the possibilities of rope-propulsion. His trainer at the Y reluctantly agreed. That spring at regionals, a promoter took him on after he'd beaten the Greater New York City standing champion. And so it was that he arrived, in the fall of 1960, in Chicago at the amateur nationals.

She was there, in the crowd, she'd made the hour-long drive over from Wheaton College. It was the first time she'd ever seen him—ever seen anyone—wrestle. That Friday night, she sat, smartly dressed with a bouquet of red roses on her lap, amid the catcalls and cheering and smoke, watching as he entered and ascended the ring, strode to the corner and disrobed. And in that moment it seemed to her that she was seeing not Spiro, not the boy she'd come so well to know, but a vision of manliness, an embodiment of purpose she herself, like a patient gardener, had cultivated, had tended from a seed, and grown. For was he not in some large measure *her* creation—made by her, meant for her—out of the diligence and longsuffering of her faith? The fruit of her prayers, watered with her tears, a shining apple her discipleship and guidance had brought forth? It hung before her now, broad-shouldered and bronze-skinned. Now had come time for the tasting.

They eloped that May, following her graduation, and moved into a small apartment in Yonkers. His career was beginning to take shape: on the New York/New Jersey circuit he was drawing larger crowds, defeating heavier and heavier opponents. The snipping of "Savior's" from the stage name was regrettable, she felt, but she understood it really wasn't marketable. As "The Human Spear" he'd still be stealthily at work, in her heart at least, as the Lord's Warrior. The addition of the nymphs disturbed her—those hired Hellenic cheerleaders—but she humored him. She knew show business was just made of that sort of thing. And you couldn't deny it, the money was really beginning to roll in: he'd made $1,000 at the Atlantic City regional championships that spring. The wedding took place there, on the Boardwalk, in an in-ring ceremony (just like Gorgeous George's), with a pipe organ, the largest in the world at the time, belting, "I'm on the Battlefield for My Lord." Rose petals fell, prefiguring their nuptial bower; like a chiffon barbell the bride was hoisted overhead and strutted triumphantly amid cheers and applause to the ring's four corners.

And then, the honeymoon, off to the Aegean, visiting the town where as a barefoot boy he'd played, who'd now returned in all his bull-like glory for his rightful inheritance of fame. And what a homecoming it was—10,000 in attendance; they recreated the ceremony in-ring; they were fêted like Olympians, the Native Son and his American—such a welcoming as Jimmy "The Golden Greek" had never seen. From island to island all through the archipelago red carpets rolled out over sunlit ivory beaches. Gladys took it all in, quietly stored it away in her heart, to ponder.

The steroids had started just after Chicago. And the amphetamine habit by now had grown into a handful-a-morning, workout-producing frenzy that left him drained for the rest of the day and needing more. None of this was known to Gladys. From her distance she watched as he swelled in celebrity and bulk—he as much as she amazed at the so-called "performance-enhancing effects" of the emerging medical science. They'd resettled on Long Island, in one of those new Space-Age communities popular after the war among the rising middle-class— that wave of first- and second-generation Greeks and Irish and Italians moving up from Queens and boroughs farther south. Nice neighbors, young professionals, seeming-decent Christian couples; trimmed lawns beginning to bubble up with children: it was just the right environ, and time, she thought, for the two of them to begin to consider having a family of their own.

What she couldn't understand, since the heydays of the honeymoon, was the direction south their bedroom life had taken. As his body, that gorgeous, rippling mass of chest and biceps, shoulders, thighs, had ballooned, other parts of him had—Well. His crumpled orchid wouldn't rouse to any of her bidding. Books and prayers, doctor visits, all to no avail. The whole thing was just as much a mystery to him— and a constant source of bitterness and shame. Who was he that he couldn't supply her with this basic biological need? What kind of a husband—what kind of *man*—with a slinky between his legs, and he just barely twenty-three? It was humiliating, nightly, to them both, to have to watch the lengths to which they'd have to go. Her repertoire of voices and scenarios, new negligee, a whole department store of scented lotions. Nothing. In the end she'd leave the bedroom, flushed and crying, with him lying on his back as if pinned, the limp and unresponsive worm curled over him, triumphant.

A private physician (also unknown to her) prescribed some topical exercises. And there was "deep relaxation," a new technique that might reduce some of the crippling professional stress and strain that most certainly were the cause. But relaxation? Who had time for that? To Spiro, it sounded like more of the same—just going soft. The doctor nodded and looked thoughtfully out the window. Perhaps . . . picture magazines? A small stack in the bedroom, if the wifey wasn't opposed, to serve as "foreplay to the foreplay," as it were . . .

The miracle was, they almost worked. Certainly to his grasping, desperate mind, it was a whole new ring of stimulus. And the fact they'd been prescribed—physician-ordered—made them, or seemed to make them, to his mind, almost licit . . . But only almost: after time and familiar failure, the old humiliation would return. And with it, a freshly fueled fluster of self-disgust—whipping himself into a frenzy over a stranger's face while his own wife lay beside him, prayerfully listening—. It was too much. They'd just have to face the fact that, apparently, it wasn't destined to happen. Gladys smiled dolefully and consoled him that it was all for the best; all things work together for good for those who love the Father. When He closes a door, He opens a window. All of this had been foreseen. Besides, weren't there already plenty of children in the world? Yes, there were, Spiro agreed. Needing *parents*, she meant. He looked at her and swallowed. "I see." As she began the adoption process, he watched in his mind the hoped-for line of manchildren slip over the horizon and fizzle in a fume of shriveled sun. Apparently his household would swell without his making. They moved on.

The whole matter had remained for years a kind of stinking swamp between them. It was something they never returned to, but something that had never been drained. It surfaced in her mind when he was away at professional matches, as more and more often now was the routine, in St. Louis or Chicago. Or Detroit. Or New Orleans. Or . . . She couldn't get those scantily clad nymphs out of her brain. Those faces from the centerfolds—how they congregated in a terrible, recurring, pestilent dream as she lay on her back in their bed, strewn now with sullied roses. How were *they* able to almost rouse him when she could not? She tried to fill the abysses of that thinking with devotion, with tearful, ardent prayers. With the children, who'd begun to arrive from the Small World Placement Agency, as to her open-armed Ark, in pairs. Ethiopia, Korea, Romania, Guatemala, China—their home became a kind of holding station for the globe, for the disfigured and displaced, damaged casualties of war and famine, a flood of hungry, scurvied, scabbed and shell-shocked souls. They occupied her through the dark hours of his travels—and the dark hours when he was there with her at home.

For he'd turned, under the increased loads of speed and steroids, into a pill-pumped bodybuilding fiend. No longer was it sufficient to be better than the best; he'd make all *future* competitors obsolete. From the iron loins of his will—his will alone—would issue a lineage of champions, Rocks and Hulks the likes of which this world had never seen. He'd forge himself into a weapon—a spear, a *missile*—of such fantastical and unimagined proportions it would require a new identity, a new name: he'd be Spiro "The Human *BOMB*."

His promoter liked it. It had chutzpah, pizzazz. Maybe "H. Bomb," for short? With some luck, they might be able to get him a booth at the World's Fair that year in Queens. Regardless, Spiro felt, this was the straight ticket in, his chance for a prime spot on the nation's screens. If he could conceive it, flesh it out, with sufficient amounts of carnage—since that's what the boys all wanted nowadays—they'd have the contract in the bag, in the *body* bag, that was—wink, wink. Spiro's mind was ablaze. All his previous training and technique for The Human Spear could easily be modified: the rope-propulsion, the fatal torso-slam—these needed only refinement, adjustment of arc and target. He'd have to find a way to strike directly from above, dropping vertically on his opponent; the perfect height, the perfect curve. And the carnage . . . Maybe he could pack himself with gobbets. Bags of pig blood or butcher-bits or. . . .

The debut was slated for the June 1965 transnationals. The venue: Olympic Auditorium in L.A.—the very ring where three years earlier Gorgeous George had been shorn by The Destroyer. What altar more befitting to stake his claim? He'd be matched against Japan—a turnip-headed, scarlet immensity of flesh called (in English) "The Enigma." He was ready. For months he'd prepared, had researched his opponent's every move. The coup de grâce he had worked to cinematic perfection; he could visualize each frame: how as he launched from the rope and arced in his ascent, tucked for the flip and whirled—a dynamo of ineluctable force and portent—climaxing now and spreading his limbs—how in that frozen moment, stilled in silent space, before the fall and the inevitable confounding of his foe, how he could feel the threads of destiny, the unbreakable strands of fate, holding him aloft—he saw it all. It was—it would be—the ne plus ultra of his career. All he had come to, packed with all he would become. Explosive potency suspended in eternal potential. *The Human Bomb.* And then: the fall.

What he hadn't anticipated: the scream. The ear-splitting horror that emitted from the giant where he stood planted below him in the ring, arms broad as skyscrapers opening to receive him, slits of eyes, his face contorted in annihilating rage. It was the sound of the sea cliffs abounding with the tongues of all the gulls of all the oceans of the world. Hatred and anguish, humiliation, vengeance—the whole tumultuous ball, the entire terrible whorl. It ripped through his sockets. His eyes went white—he saw his shadow, like a crumpled silken kerchief on the floor, as he fell and fell, and seemed to fall forever, through the hole that made that roar . . .

The whole disaster had been caught on national television, of course. Among the millions of viewers in the vast American dark sat Gladys in Long Island, having put the children to bed, gripping the damask seat of their sofa. He would view it himself, replay it over the years, over and over during the miserable months to come, as he lay in Mount Sinai's surgical ward, in traction. The splinters in his spine had been removed, the cord and column realigned. The tongs in his skull that attached to the halo-vest kept him suspended, floating in and out of time. Respiratored, spastic and incontinent—conditions only worsened by the amphetamine withdrawal—when Gladys wheeled him out in six months' time, he looked like a washed-up towel. He was twenty-five. He felt like an eighty-year-old man. The future was over. *Tetelestai*. He would never wrestle again.

He did for a time try his hand as a promoter. He was invited, on his celebrity's receding wave, to speak at a number of children's charities and hospitals, spearheading various fundraising campaigns. He made the token appearance at the Hellenic Society holiday functions. Nothing satisfied. The City reminded him of a grave. The autumn streets at evening whispered with the leaves of forgotten triumph. It was time; he, too, would leave. It had been quite the honeymoon, quite the odyssey. But what of all that now? It was a Cyclops' cave. That winter they packed house and moved with the children to the place all odysseys end.

To Ithaca.

+

The man bending over the clogged pool pump was troubled. The girl who had come to lay out in the sun by the poolside while he worked had removed her top. He was struggling not to appear to notice; it was important to him, given the situation, that he not appear to notice. But the girl was watching him closely, he could feel it, behind her oversized sunglasses. She had begun to appear each week now as he worked, to watch him closely. Some weeks she sat on the pool ledge, dangling her legs into the water, her legs that were spread a little too widely not to invite notice, reading a paperback novel, though he could feel it then, too, she was watching him closely. She hadn't moved as he'd brushed by her with the net; she just sat there, silently, apparently, engrossed. He'd had to work the net around and over her.

But now she lay on the poolside, far enough away from the edge that if he needed to step around to the side near where she lay, to work, he could, without . . . involving her? (But she was already involved.) Confronting her? Engaging her? He wasn't sure what the word, but he knew it was very important, given the delicacy of the situation, that he not allow himself to appear to be doing any of those things.

But this was his pool, after all. There needed to be some rules. You couldn't just let it all hang out and go back to Woodstock whenever you wanted, could you? But he knew the girl enough (she'd lived with them for five years now) to know that the last thing you wanted with her, with this girl, in this kind of situation, would be to act as if there were some kind of problem with this kind of behavior. Which would give her the advantage, the upper hand. He could picture her reaction: Could you please put that back on, he'd ask, and she'd appear to be indignant or confused. Why, she'd say. It doesn't turn you on, does it? Aren't you supposed to be my "father?"

She was always doing things like that. Provoking him. Messing with his head. Leaving the door wide open while she was taking a shower. Sitting at the kitchen counter eating an apple, barely clad. None of the other girls had ever done anything like that. Certainly none of them had left him notes. *I want your rocket cock so high inside me I can taste it.* That wasn't fair. That just wasn't fair at all. Even if it was written in her journal, she'd intentionally left it open for him to find.

As now it wasn't fair: how she had made this her Sunday afternoon routine, coming to lay out by the pool while he worked while his wife was away at Bible study. Did she think he didn't know? Did she think he didn't see it? The whole scheme was perfectly, transparently clear. She knew they'd be alone. She knew she would have him in her sights—herself in his, rather—and there was nothing he could do. Powerless to cause a scene, powerless to appear to notice. If he were another type of man, he might actually enjoy it.

He had honestly hoped the last one would *be* the last—Lucy, a homely, unassuming eleven-year-old from China, whom they'd had to release due to ungovernable night terrors. Thirty-seven of them, over these thirty-something years, had taken it out of him. He had been looking forward to the consolations of age and the peace of mind that comes with oblivion. Honestly speaking, he was emotionally drained. Nothing had really satisfied, personally or professionally, over the years; even the pool business had come to seem to him more of the same, just the last in a line of entrepreneurial disappointments. Sure, it had paid the bills and kept the foster cupboards stocked; he'd been able to keep it afloat for longer than any of the other ventures. Poseidon Pool Service, with its trident design reminiscent of a spear, had certainly seen more success than the 1970s franchise, Spiro's Gyros. Still. He'd never, since the accident, felt himself as anything other than adrift. Directionless. Detached. People swam into and out of his life like the children, the world that flowed randomly into and out of their home; nobody stuck, nobody ever emerged from the purposefully opened shades or a reflective kitchen window, content to remain in the weekly game of watching him, anonymous, watching them. Watching, he felt, though never himself really ever actually seen.

She had seen him. Something in him was certain of it. In these moments of secret and illicit confrontation (yes, that *was* the word) she was *engaging* him, like a skillful and sly opponent, searching out the recesses and sources of his strength. And the weak points that inevitably surrounded it, like sleepy sentries, breaches in the wall—: She was presenting him with (what else?) a test of will. A clear, seductive pool in which he might immerse himself. Or not. She was herself already halfway in the shallows. He'd just begun to dip his toenail in. Would he engage her? From the ropes, or from full-center in the ring? He glanced up as she rolled away from him, reaching for her glass of Coke. He had that choice. The water between them burned like a low blue fume.

Over the next few days he watched her carefully. Nothing. No indication of the secret between them like a shared, forbidden ring. She moved aloof through the routine laid out for her by his wife—sweeping and cleaning, restocking the canteen—without so much as a word, without ever lifting an eye, until he himself could almost be fooled that everything was otherwise. But of course they weren't alone. He knew the silent provocations being prepared, even beneath her purposefully unflattering clothes; that underneath the knee-length, shapeless nightshirts were taut and finely honed stratagems being hatched, assembled and laid out, stewing in time, becoming ripe for the unveiling. Only once, once only, did he catch a glimpse of the magnitude to come. It was mealtime, the three of them at the table. While his wife was saying the prayer, he opened his eyes and . . . God, the glare confronting him—an unflinching amalgam of mockery and resolve, icy defiance, ferocity of purpose ... He shuddered a little and quickly lowered his head. She was prepared.

That Sunday, as expected, she appeared. He kept at his work, even whistling a little, skimming the deep end for insects and fallen debris. She chose a chair, dragged it clangingly up to the pool's edge, reclined the back with a crash and flopped herself across the vinyl straps. There. What an entrance. The top, he remarked, had returned. Two symmetrical, mermaid-reminiscent scallop cups. That was a development, a welcome one. It indicated balance. Moderation. That she was beginning to sense the strength that resides in restraint. As if intuiting his thoughts, she brought her thumbs down under the cups, lifted them to expose a twinned lunulae of white, held them there for a moment and then let them settle again in place. He sighed. She was showing herself a truly worthy opponent. A wise child, mature beyond her years, and knowing. Pulling out the paperback from the previous week, she began to pretend to read (the oversized sunglasses perched precariously on her button nose), while with her other hand, seeming absentmindedly, she began to slide the string of her neck strap towards him away from its knot—stretching it slowly taut, closer and closer each time—and letting it drop.

It was getting hot. The afternoon sun was bleeding through the oaks and falling across the pool in rippling mottled globs of molten gold. He coughed. Immediately, she froze, seemed to become erect at the sound, the tightened string between her fingers an antenna, over which droned the hum of the pump and the cicadas' distant screaming. He, too, stood motionless, the pole mid-stroke, his head on fire. Something was on the verge of happening. The knot at her neck, he could swear, had begun to slip. The butterfly bow had almost closed its wings. Just as he was about to call to her to *Wait! Stop*—*!* he heard the sound of violent rattling. (*What's* *this? What's this?*) She lifted her wrist, looked at her gummy watch and smiled as the wooden gate to the yard swung open.

Eternity could not have prepared him for what was ushered in. In stripes of neon and fluorescent polka-dots—where they weren't, that was, covered entirely in their own skin—five nubile virgins bounded over the lawn to the squeals of delighted and elated expectation. A *pool party? Girlfriends from the church?* He didn't know; his wife would never have allowed it. She rose and began to caper among them, giggly and frolicsome, as one by one they hurled themselves into the water. So this was what she'd brought him. (He'd withdrawn into the shadows of the oaks.) This was what in her silence she'd prepared—procured—the water now a frothing, agitated mass of gasps and orgiastic flailing. He took his pole and carried it back to the equipment shed. How would he meet her challenge? Would he change into a suit himself and stride, godlike, among them? Or was the better course—he'd taken out the chlorine testing kit—to show himself immune, aloof and unaffected, Olympus-es above her low-blow scheme? Or perhaps unappeased, disapproving of her offering . . . Girding his loins, he exited the shed, walked to the poolside where a trio of them was gathered. Undaunted, without an iota of acknowledgement, he stooped and dipped the test tube, directly and deliciously, into their copper-bellied, oiled, oblivious midst.

As he lifted the litmus to the light, he caught her eye, watching him from the shallows. What was that look? Was she acknowledging his prowess? Approving? Cautiously assaying? Eyeing him sardonically for a slip? He couldn't tell before her goggled face slid under.

Later that week she tested him again, with greater boldness—and coldness. He was lying in bed, his wife beside him, both asleep, when he was awakened by the sound, outside, of heavy moaning. Light rhythmic, rippling noises coming from the pool. Stifled whispering and groans. Before he could move, his wife shot from the bed and bolted out of the room. They ceased soon after, the sounds, but he could imagine their sources, and it pained him to know they weren't intended fully for him. How different, and how much worthier an opponent she had been, had she brought that all out into the daylight, for him to see.

It left him smaller. Not just the knowledge that, now, there was another—a competitor on whom she'd devote (for instance) her journal—and divide her time—but that, in those moments of overhearing their gross, unbridled pleasure (in *his* pool, no less), he'd been forced against his will to participate in it, in and on the terms of the competitor. It was as if in listening to her body being touched by hands not his, he'd had to imagine *himself* touching her in places, and in ways, that would overcome, out-shadow and negate those other hands. It was as if, in a way (and this was the thing that pained him), a vital piece of him had been torn away and had in some diminished sense *become* the Other.

But mostly what hurt was that they couldn't go on as before. No. The terms had shifted. If he was now no longer entirely who he was— as she no longer was entirely her (his) own—there was no meaningful way, without a fundamental change, for the two of them to continue to engage. New stratagems and tactics, an overhaul of armor, unprecedented methods of resistance and attack: these must be the means by which he'd have to compensate, and more than compensate, for the development—or, rather, lack. The age was debased; he accepted that. Salacious audiences who wanted only shock-and-awe. Bigger guns, bigger phalluses, quivering tubs of guts and gore. He'd forge a new wonder, from the tawdry gear she'd forced him to put on. No more stealth, no more surreptitious gazing. Done with dawdling; so long, sweet restraint. He was coming, head-on, straight into her center (what she'd wanted): *Rocket Cock*. The Ravisher.

When he looked back now over those few whirling, final days, it seemed to him he moved through a kind of amniotic montage—driving the van from strangers' pools to pools, performing his services, though himself not fully present. In his mind he sifted through the years; images, long forgotten or suppressed, came back to him in their embryonic bones and brightness. Gorgeous George at the Garden, 1949. The triumphant homecoming in Argos. Nymphs in faux satin (one, Lola, doe-eyed) tossing roses over fleeces of platinum and gold. They bobbed in memory like a dreamy archipelago of design and valediction. For he felt it, at his core, he was sailing out, into the final mirage. All his life had been a grainy gathering of waves on the horizon: what drove him towards it wasn't who he was, but some future other whom he might become. In his fibers and sinews, he knew himself a sad and failing fact; but in the blood of an Idea—in a spear, in a bomb—it was *there* he was reborn. It had always been so. Since as a boy he stood outside the Garden, listening himself inside the crowd. Then as now. Life was elsewhere. As on some silver screen, he had always lived somehow outside himself.

The Crusade: it, too, came back. Ages (a God) ago, unreal—the Garden where the wandering Adam, he, dewy with tears, had been born again. The evangelist's voice had sounded, had summoned a new creature. Through the thousands he'd stepped forward—and still he stepped. He saw himself at seventeen, swimming now with all the others, all the other creatures that his self had been, bobbing in hazy brightness of a womb. They all were present. All eternally becoming. Here at the end, they'd make him room. He'd strip his sack of skin and leave it at the pool's edge. Then slide his soul, like a shimmering silver rod, completely in.

+

She had been confined to her room after the incident, instructed to pray droplets of sweat and blood. Her meals were eaten behind the padlocked door. He'd seen her once, at evening, as she was released to empty her bucket. In the hallway's lurid fluorescence she looked like a beaten dog. He watched as she moved mechanically past, without lifting her eyes, and entered the bathroom. Her battered hand compliantly pulled the door.

Nothing of this guise, of course, deceived him. He'd heard the night-long hammerings, the rage balled up in those screams. There wasn't a sliver of will in her that was broken. The stains on her nightshirt, those spoke of a fury, he knew, far beyond mere vomited bile. The dried slime encrusting her chin was the froth of a demon's unleashing.

Which was why, that Saturday night, at his wife's insistence, they entered her room to pray. No typical table-grace, this; no adoration of the Virgin. The Enemy had announced himself in her flesh, his wife claimed. They must put on the Lord's full armor. This would require the laying-on of hands, supplication in fiery Pentecostal tongues; it would require, said his wife, physical restraint, pinning her down till the evil be expunged. They'd begin at her feet and proceed slowly up to her head, applying the lash prayerfully at every point, till they located the crevice of that festering Hell inside her and hounded its occupant out.

A flurry swept through his chest. So it had come, he thought, and this was how it had come. He stood at the door while his wife worked the lock, his mind filled with blackest imaginings. *It had come.* There was only one end. Destiny is destiny because it is not otherwise. It fits your shape precisely as your skin. Through a hazy maze, you open the door, you are gradually allowed to see it: the end is You—the final mirage congealed into your shape and substance. You open the door (he saw it). You stride to the bedside where awaits, laid out as on an altar strewn with aromatic gobbets, what thing You finally are. You must take it in your arms, you must wrap yourself inside it, and you must be the sacrificial fire. The end is the end because it is not otherwise. It is the final ravishment by fire.

The whites of her eyes rolled back in her head. His weight on her chest, the whole of him. A highflown hammering of bells, bells beating, the tongues of bells, in his head. He was Jacob with the angel. Jonah with the whale. Jehovah in the sockets of the wind. A surge of electric jelly from the sky (he closed his eyes), blue agony, (at last) a joy . . . When it was over, he lay exhausted upon her as if washed up on a distant ivory shore. Wave after wave pulled over his thighs, and in the distance, the meretricious mewing of gulls. The sound of his wife's low weeping in the corner: a confused muttering of prayers, gulls' gibberish. He lifted himself to his elbows and gazed down on her. Her ecstasy was still.

By the following Sunday she'd be funneled back into the system; the lustrous pool was drained. His heart felt crumpled, like it'd lost its center. He prayed to God he'd never see her face again.

SENECA

I

You lie in the lidless, pallid light of five a.m., the day—another inconceivable day—against you. Against it, your tired mind tosses a few tentative shapes like the stems of Ophelia's broken-up bouquet: heart's ease, columbine, rue—a little cluster of seductive improbabilities. You could die, for instance. You could never rise from these Egyptian 1,000-thread-count cotton sheets. Your children could find you in an hour finally, imperviously useless to their needs. You take some relish in imagining their discovery: at first they'll think it some perverse happy game—"Shake Mommy Awake!"—stretch her into shape—before turning mindlessly to ransack the room. You listen to their proddings from your novel distance, their voices like little vitriolic birds; "The children are up," your husband will mutter, as if this were ever news—as if those words were the stimulant you've salivated for all night, and now, rising and reentering the domestic cage, can murmur, *Thank you, my wise and beneficent jailer.* Or not— seeing as you're the one who's dead. That brief, unprecedented luxury is enough to fill your hateful little heart with praise.

Eventually you will rise, of course, make the coffee, make the break- fasts and the lunches. Drop the children off. Drive to your humiliat- ing job. In the cramped cube you share with another faculty adjunct, you'll have an orphaned hour to adopt. There's the paper you'll deliver this weekend at the conference on philosophy in Canada. There's still the morning lecture to prepare. The lecture hall rotunda will resemble a giant fishbowl where 150 stone-eyed guppies stare. The dwindling autumn maples in the windows are your mother, who disappeared in a maple-brilliant haze when you were twelve. Her name now, conveniently, is Autumn; she's living with her guru, Alan, God knows where. Peru, it was, last time you saw her, in Albany, in that dreamcatcher-coffee shop. The Farm's Twelve Tribes had become "untenable," she told you; they were heading south to found the "neo-pagan Camelot." Little intermittent burbles from a fountain in the corner mingled with the aroma of patchouli and bat shit . . .

Your mother has never met your children. And you're fairly sure she doesn't know of Livvie's death—Livvie, your ebullient older sister who succumbed last spring to a tumor in the brain. You always envied her—her sureness of instinct, that whiplash-crack of a laugh, her facility with horses. It occurs to you now in death that you envy her still. It occurs to you that since your mother doesn't know, she is in some Schrödinger's-cat sense still living. But then your mother doesn't know that you're not dead, so what's the difference?

You sigh, and the ghost of a tear wells in your eye. *Really?* you ask. Has it come to this? The wonder of the world, its promise, its unutterable wash of mystery and stars—where did it all go? Once you were larger than this. Once life felt, well, alive. Not this morbid interminable treadmill of, what?—insipid whatlessness. You search the sleep-deprived ruin of your mind for something generative, something to *press* against, some paradox, a surprising dialectic. Please God just one thought worthy of a thought! And your tired mind turns up: sand. Nothing but time-wasted, distinction-withering sand stretching infinitely away on the horizon, to a wavy mirage (hello) who happens to be you—or the you you once had planned—before you asked the universe for *just one small thing* to make your petty little life distinctive, and the universe, with consummate irony, delivered: twins.

It has occurred to you to kill them. Never a thought that you would act upon, of course, but you have had it. You've read your Medea, been suitably appalled by those "monsters" on the evening news—mothers with their station wagons backed into lakes, hairdryers dropped into tubs at bath time, who just "found themselves confused." And the thought has come to you, upon innumerable playgrounds, small-talking with innumerable Volvo moms, with their palaver about skim lattes and some health craze called "Pilates," that the monster is not so foreign. There is such a thing, you've told yourself, as self-preservation. Certain actions are pardonable as self-defense. Propagation of the species need not entail, for Christ's sake, mental retardation.

Oh shut up, you tell yourself and sigh, rolling over and yanking the sheets up over your head. A whole half-hour now wasted, thinking about them. Under the cool cotton tent you hear your husband breathing, ensconced in his geometric dream of prismatic towers and aquariums aswim with mermaids of titanium. (The brooding-genius architect: ask him.) You smell him. Nothing discernible. You nose closer and smell him again. You're certain he's having an affair, he must be. No one could be that happy in this house without an add-on.

She comes to you, hazily: his intern graduate student, twenty-four and tight-chested. High cheekbones, still unflagging jowls, star-eyed, idealistic—. That's what kills. That's the biggest betrayal. She's a goddamned version of your younger self. The you you were when you still could hold a room with conversation. You, ebullient over a glass of Chardonnay, the you who knew her mind and knew how in a flash to articulate it. God, you saw it then—the direction of the world and what your Columbia coterie could do to change it. Teach *thought*. Teach *clear thinking*. Teach *philosophy*. That was 1982. Ten years since Autumn-Mama disappeared into the maple-colored haze. And now, ten years later, where are we? Where are *you*? . . . Exactly. You close your eyes and sink into the haze of 1,000-thread-count cotton. In that cool Lethean current you can lose yourself and breathe. At the edge of the world, there's the sound of tiny footsteps hurrying forward. You cover your ears and fill your gills, dive deep—

+

After lecture, a student lingers. You will have expected it. Predictably, it's the dark boy, Dominic, whose mind is on fire with Plato. Dominic, with the thoughtful green eyes, in his seat in the back of the lecture hall, top row, center. Can he come to your office hours again today, please? Yes, of course, you tell him. You'll be there, as usual. In the cube. He smiles. He knows where to find you.

You'll lug your bag and armful of books from the rotunda down the shimmeringly bland system of tiles to where they end in a darkened cul de sac of doors. You unlock one and step inside. Immediately you feel the fingers at your throat: *Time.* How much do you have while the room's still yours, while you sit at the desk piled with someone else's clutter, someone else's groundbreaking research, the photos on the sill from someone else's Caribbean vacation? You sigh and spread a place for yourself at the desk, pull out a set of papers from your bag: your presentation for the conference. The conference on religion and phi-losophy this weekend in Toronto. You'd rather have the plague. You can already picture the swollen phalluses of the keynote speakers; around them, in crashing, ejaculatory waves, the sycophantic swarms spuming, clinging, desperate for a name, any name. Endless panels participants presenters all alike all anonymous—and you among them. Some ardent adjunct lecturer from (where was it again?) Ithaca. Another mouth expounding rarefied palaver, a titillating abstraction its speaker doesn't even believe. And why are you going? Why are you giving it? To make yourself more marketable, of course. To attempt to secure eventually a university position more dignified and lucrative than Adjunct Whore.

You don't need the money, as your husband is fond of reminding you. You take that verity as the poison it is. It makes your debilitating professional anxiety all that much more ludicrous. You don't *need* to do anything. You could stay in bed all day drinking pink Cosmopolitans, watching reruns of *Days of Our Lives*. You could take up Pilates (many do, apparently), sip skim lattes at Bread & Circus with the other well-off, jobless wives. The point is, you have elected your prison. You have created your own professional hell. And you sustain it every second you persist in the illusory—what? ... (*think! think!*) empty shell: the empty shell on the shore of the Ocean of Unlikelihood, the dream better left behind, of *one day* making a life of the languishing crustacean that used to be called your mind.

There's a knock at the door. It's probably your officemate. She usually comes around now to collect her piles of research. The department's rising star. No surprise, she has no children. But, no, it's the dark boy, Dominic, whose head pokes hopefully around the corner. Dominic, with the peacock-green eyes. You sigh and slide your pile of papers to the side of the desk. Come in, come in. He's come today to talk with you again about Plato and the origin of human sexuality. How the soul, he'll rehash from lecture, originally one, was divided by Eros into masculine and feminine—and a third, hermaphroditic, you'll add, but he's far gone—the severed soul, cut off, forever seeking its lost sister— thoughts young Dominic says he's always had but didn't have words for until Plato dreamed them into form. You smile at his solecism. At the ardor of his thoughts, which makes his eyes, green embers, assume an even deeper green. If that were possible. He reminds you of yourself in some prehistoric life, and you're surprised at your sudden urge to reach and lay your hand across his knee. You don't, of course. You clear your throat and tell him, in your most convincing professorial tone, that, yes, these ideas are very old. Clichés almost, part of the DNA of how we think. A collective cultural consciousness. You look at the ceiling. A kind of human memory bank. Ah, he says, turning his gaze to the single office window, with its view of a dark brick wall and fire escape. *A bank of human memory. Yes, I have thought that, too.*

But today Dominic isn't here to talk about Plato. Dominic's an anthropology major, a junior; next semester, he hopes to conduct study abroad, in Honduras, in the coastal city of Trujillo. It's where he's from, he tells you, where his family still lives; it's been a very long time since he's seen them or been home. Sounds nice, you say, Honduras. Your eyes wander to the photo on the sill. A strange man stands on a white beach holding a blue, umbrellaed drink. He smiles, a line of Kennedy-brilliant teeth. A line of vibrant blue-green coils and uncoils behind him. There are birds of Paradise and wild orchids and what looks like an ancient banyan tree. It's very poor, says Dominic. Not like the photographs. Of course, you say and find his eyes again. It rarely is. But in Honduras, he continues, there is the site of a very famous Mayan temple, deep in the western jungle, near the border of Guatemala. The anthropology group would be studying there for a week, with professional archaeologists! It's the chance of a lifetime, a chance to get to know the ruins firsthand, he says. *And* the mysteries inside them . . . He leans in. His enthusiasm, raw and adolescent, is nonetheless endearing. You listen, half amused, as he embarks on the more gruesome details of human sacrifice—flayed virgins, priests wrapping themselves into the warm, slick skins; the quick incision, the fist thrust deep into the chest, drawing out the still quivering heart. Of course, you tell him. No question about the benefits. Theory into praxis. Would you be willing to write a statement of support on his behalf? he asks. He needs a recommendation from a faculty member; you've seen his enthusiasm about the class, in lectures, in these office-hour conversations. They're looking for something from someone who knows you well.

You think for a moment. There's something about these requests that always triggers the cynic in you. Is this what all that was about? A recommendation? The opportunity, yet another, to be used? You would love it if the free exchange of ideas were ever simply that: free, with no ulterior strings attached. No need for the wandering of thought to venture anywhere other than itself: just two people sitting in a room, freely talking. That's *philosophy* . . .

But this is college. You know that. It's a market people are paying for—though you're sure Dominic is on scholarship—and there are practical realities, professional expectations over and above whatever intellectual pleasantries blah blah blah. You know this. Still. You wonder why no one has ever offered to write a recommendation for *you*—to get out, to go somewhere, the "chance of a lifetime." Even destitute Honduras, for a weekend, living the photographic dream . . . It's a petty little moment that you savor while he sits there, bright-eyed and hopeful, before you give your answer—which of course will be yes—: a little door, hanging open, into another possibility . . . And what if you said something else?

What if you said, for instance, "Actually, Dominic, I *don't* know you that well. Why don't we have a long martini lunch, see where that takes us?" Lunch. That's something students and professors do. "Maybe dinner and a movie." That's pushing it. You glance at his hands. Long, slim, dark fingers. How about we go for something really outlandish?

"Actually, Dominic, what if we took the weekend getting to know each other *really* well, holed up together, say, in your apartment?" You imagine for a moment what that might be. A dingy, sink-stinking hovel. Roommates—international—certainly. "Or a hotel." He'll look at you, innocently puzzling. You'll wink and reassure him: "I'll pay." Then he sees it. He points at you and smiles. *La profesora has a sense of humor.* But you're not smiling. You hold his gaze. A long, green silence opens in the room between you.

+

On Friday morning your husband drops you at the airport. The children have been deposited, everything's been arranged—the food for the weekend compartmentalized and labeled, the vitamins laid out, the hydra-headed loads of laundry folded and put away. Have a good time at the conference, he tells you. Good luck with the panel. It's not about luck and having a good time, you say. It's about having an opportunity for once to exercise your mind. He lets out a characteristically bewildered sigh. You know what I mean. Just . . . do your best. I intend to, you tell him, and take your bags from the back seat and slam the door. You watch the Audi make its beeline for the exit. Have a good time yourself, you say.

A few moments later, a motorcycle will pull up. You'll strap your bag and briefcase to the sides and mount, making wry note of the brand name on the gas tank: *Triumph.* Why does the woman always have to ride in back, you think, as the kickstand pops and the throttle jerks you into gear. But it's a passing irritation in the exhilarating, sudden rush.

Where we heading? he calls over his shoulder as you come to the airport exit. The sky is wide, a cloudless camisole of blue. There's a brisk autumn chill and a lingering haze in the maples, smoldering like vermilion embers on the hills. The road winds in front of you like the tail of a chameleon and slips invisibly around a bend. You tighten your grip on the sides of his leather jacket and put your mouth to his ear.

Just drive till I say when.

You're taking him, of all places, to the cabin owned by your family up in the Finger Lakes, on Seneca. It hasn't been used since Livvie's death. Or has it? You have the sudden suspicion that your sister, Emma, might be using it that weekend with her family. But wouldn't she have called to check? You don't know. It's doubtful. And besides, you've fallen a little out of touch. Still. You should give her a call when you arrive—if she's not already *there*. You shake your head. Stupid. Just stupid. Careless. But then, what would *Emma* care? Emma, with her banker husband, Paul, three kids and those brainless yellow Labs, living in Bronxville in their million-dollar penthouse, where she shops and plays tennis for a living. She'd probably think it an amusing eccentricity, you and your Latino motorcycle lover, an indication of the profound dissatisfaction in your life that she's always known was there. You with your serious-ness, your middle-daughter brooding, your "philosophy." Really, Anya, who has time for those things? Why bother yourself with thinking? What's thinking going to change? Look at Livvie. Did she ever think in the end she'd have a brain tumor?

You picture her at the funeral. Emma, decked to the nines, look-ing like Jackie Onassis. As if, what, she was going to pick somebody up? Some teenage crush—one of Livvie's high-school boyfriends? Or, more likely, one of his strapping teenaged sons. You know that she has lovers. She's told you all about them—the pedigreed young studs she has delivered when Paul's not home. (This, confessed over a post-funeral Sex on the Beach at Applebee's.) *Honey, all I have to do is pick up the phone.* Her favorite thing's to do it in their shower—so many mirrors! It's like there's seven of you there, all getting it at once. It's better than therapy, you can see yourself from so many different angles. And you don't even have to talk to anyone! Anya, she tells you, you should do a little something for yourself. I can't imagine what your life must be with those two twins. Look at your hair! It's gone and lost its luster. And your *skin*. Let me set you up with some special cream. She's baffled by your nondescript attire: God, Darling, if I went beige, where would I be? Lost in the wash. Paul would forget me in a heartbeat. And I hate to remind you, but it's still the twentieth century. We women need our men . . .

Ugh.

Still, you'd better call her. Best to have no surprises. You turn your eyes back to the road and see a gas station coming up, lean your head over his shoulder: Pull in here. From the payphone you watch him as he paces around the bike and stretches. Long, sinewy limbs; as they lift, beneath his T-shirt where it rises, the strip of tight bronze skin. A Grecian figure, athletic silhouette, like on the urns . . . A voice beats in your ear. Hello? *Hello?* Yes, Anya. You should do a little something for yourself.

Emma, it figures, has a fundraising dinner tonight with Paul, and the kids have weekend tennis camp. But what a great idea, she tells you. Sisters' night out at the old place! You two should definitely do that sometime. You tell her you knew it was a long shot but, hey, you were going, by yourself, just to unwind, and wanted to check. That's really sweet of you, Anya, she says. Really thoughtful. I'd like that. Me, too, Emma, you lie.

Back on the bike, he asks you how much farther. At this distance, the woods have grown thick along the highway's single lane; like the hackles of some great dark animal they crouch, threatening to lurch forward. Not far, you tell him. We're almost there. He guns the engine and you feel the thrill of the cool air rushing your nostrils, whipping your lusterless hair. Your fingers on his ribs, this novel nearness, the feel of his spine pressed between your breasts. You watch for a time your shadows flying beside you, joined at the hip. When you look up, you find the old view of the road now divided by his youthful head. It's all so dizzying. You concentrate your vision on his nape, where the clipped hair comes together in two perfect little whorls.

+

Childhood, it's your hand that moves forward now, mysteriously enough, to open the rough screen door; your eyes that meet the sheeted figures of the furniture standing in the room, spectral ancestors, impassive, impenetrable in their almost totem solitude, the way they were in life: Grandfather, his head a ruffled hawk's, reading in that chair, his eyeless eyes, the spectacles in lamplight, little discs of molten gold; Oma, a tall clematis, a flourishing vine of bone, the bone-white flower of her face so seldom opening (although once: you drew a stack of photographs from the stairwell drawer—who was the boy in Kodachrome sitting on the porchswing, standing on the lake in a canoe, in front of the garden that no longer was a garden?—she snapped the pictures from your hands and closed the drawer, but just before she turned you saw the tear at her eye, a gleaming bead of solder): they were your twin-portals to the world of silence, to the magnitude of all that must not be said, to towering confusions and the depthless private spiralings long summer afternoons beside the rippling ministry of water. Seneca. Osininka. Oas-in-in Ka. You asked your father once about the name and how it was that Seneca the Younger of the book there on the shelf was the same, proud of your discovery, something Latin that would please him, precocious link between his foreign readings and this familiar place. No. No, Anya. No again. And sinking back to his unbothered occupation with the ancients.

Days you drifted, making faery houses out of moss and birchbark, admiring spiders on the outside kitchen screen, watching from the shore the two of them row out . . . Could you come, too? No, Anya. Clumsy with a paddle. No, no. Look at Livvie. Jesus Christ, girl, can't you sit still? In the middle! You'll tip the boat . . . Always in the middle. And the two of them, always rowing out, together—the daughter and the son he always wanted, never had.

It all comes back now with the heavy saturation of home movies: Livvie on a bike, Livvie as an acrobat, Livvie after Livvie riding horses. And you, at the margins, holding the new baby, trying hard to don a winning, memorable smile. And Mother—Mama—before her name is Autumn—in animated conversation with a glass of wine. It must be 1965. You're five, Livvie seven. Seven years until the seasons permanently change. Before your mother and the maples assume their brilliant, brainwashed haze. Disciples of Yahshua, only Son of God; the Twelve lost Tribes of The Farm. Oh, how she bought it. Hook, line and sinker. (Osininka) And then: one late October, with the dwindling leaves, she'll leave. The man behind the camera becomes a stonier stone. And God becomes too real to be believed. The cabin will be closed to all but spiders, the spectral ancient ones will pass away. High school will happen, the scatterings of college . . . On a day in 1980 he'll call to say he's moving to Florida—take the cabin, the house in Albany, divide them as you three see fit—he'll be on a houseboat in Sarasota if you want him where he'll wear away on Tanqueray and fish. And it's true: last time you see him, at Livvie's funeral, he looks like a worn-out shoe—gin-pickled and salt-crusted, baked face of shrunken leather, his eyes a lost, horizonless Delft blue.

You open the door. The screen ghosts snigger in the squeaking of the spring and withdraw, exhaling must and mothballs, as the gnomon of sunlight enters. It falls across the floor where dust motes twirl like deep-sea bubbles over sheeted mounds of coral. Your shadows swim to the center of the room and hold. Over there, you tell him. He takes the bags and puts them in a corner. You point him down in the direction of the dock. Wait for me there.

When was the last time you were here, the three of you, sisters? The summer before last? The summer before last spring, to celebrate the successful treatment coming out of Jacksonville. She was back, she and Tom, living for the summer in the New York apartment. The doctors at the Center had granted the release, a vacation, for "quality of life." She was, as ever, optimistic. There's nothing about this hurdle we can't canter right across, she laughed. As if it all, all of it, her whole cancer-riddled life, were just a horse. You knew better, in your typical cynical way, how her meager airborne months were marked.

So that was it. She'd insisted—all of you, all three families, all the kids, the dogs—you all come up here together. It'd be just like old times, a full cabin, lots of laughter, stories, fireside games. Right, you thought. Clearly, Livvie, you have no children. Lots of mindless chasing toddlers around so they don't drown, lots of trying to keep Emma's brats from killing one another, killing the dogs, trying to get them all at a reasonable hour to bed. That room, the kids' old room, that was the worst. Three bunkbeds, full of your and Emma's spawn, like monkeys, trashing it every night into the wee hours. "Oh let up, Anya"—this over another countless glass of wine. "Leave them alone. Don't you remember? It's how *we* used to be." Exactly, Emma. And that's the problem with parenting: you replicate yourself. And the parents, vis-à-vis *vous*, have become the infants again.

But you went, you all came, captives to Livvie's will; you had no choice. And the husbands, predictably, played golf. And the womenfolk, trapped in the nineteenth century all over, stayed chained to the children in the kitchen. Is this what you learned at law school, Livvie? you wanted to ask her. Finger-painting? Is this the doctors' "quality of life?" Is this really how you want to remember your remaining moments on this planet? Punching fucking paper dolls? But you didn't. And you know perfectly well why not. She'd have turned to you with her chemo-bloated face, the patch over her eye to match her dwindling patch of hair, and have answered in that withering, unwavering, envied voice you've known your whole pathetic, petty life: *Yes, Anya. It is. Yes.*

And then, nine months later, you were there. (You can see the branch of rock from your position in the room through the window where it stretches into the lake.) Scattering her ashes in the water.

He was there. Drained and soulless. You didn't open the house, you all just came and drove away. Your last memory of him: a stone-still silhouette, facing out across the water. Where they would row, now all a rippling, all-obliterating blaze.

It's time. You take off your conference clothes, change into a warm sweater and jeans and walk down to the dock to join him. He's coming out of the water as you approach. Isn't it freezing? you ask. He shakes the lake out of his hair and hangs back on the ladder and smiles. Youth. Your sunbright, streaming, bronze Adonis. It's then you see the scar—a transverse purple ridge arcing down across his abdomen to his waistband, where it disappears under his pin-striped boxers. An almost perfect crescent. As if it had been drawn by a tusk or claw. What happened there? you ask. He climbs out, dries himself with his shirt and takes a seat beside you on the dock. The trees across the lake describe a calm reflection of themselves in the leafgreen water.

He tells you of his childhood in Trujillo, the coastal city, where his father still works as a spearfisherman. How as a boy, he loved to go with his older brother snorkeling among the reefs. The colors, he says. They are surreal under the water. They make you feel the rest of your life you're colorblind. Those reds, he says, pointing out at the late-October russet in the oaks. Underwater they would be like lungs of fire—like luminarias, lit from within. With tiny capillaries of blues and greens, like peacock tails, trembling with tips of gold.

I see, you say, looking out. The low iron clouds behind make them seem to leap forward across the water like caged tigers in bas-relief.

Up here the colors are old, he continues. They've been looked at too long. Too long, with too many people living on top of each other.

You give a smirk. Don't you have plenty of people, too, living on top of each other in overpopulated Central America?

He looks at you and smiles. It's not the same, he says. It's a different . . . *relación*. He spreads his hands and gestures across the water. With the sea. Always changing, always new. It's like waking every morning underwater. She keeps us young inside her.

She?

He turns to look at you. Yemayá. The great sea mother. We still worship her, many of us. With the Virgin.

Oh God, you think and roll your eyes. The kid's a True Believer. Pretty soon it'll be Autumn all over again. You picture them, her and Alan, hirsute and naked, traipsing brainlessly across the Andes. Aboriginal Mama. Some great one *she* turned out to be . . .

You were going to tell me about that scar.

He smiles and looks down. My father says I'm always getting distracted. He crosses his legs and leans over the edge of the dock, looking down into the water. They were spearfishing, he tells you, he and his brother, out over the reefs one morning. He had dived into the coral and was exploring below. His brother, thinking it was clear, let loose at a school of passing mackerel. As Dominic leapt to ascend, he felt the spear.

You imagine him in that moment, stunned, limbs limp, the unspooling thread of blood. You see him as from below, where he's a silhouette against the bright rippling sky. A jet-black constellation in a spreading nebula of red, lit from within, hemmed by unending greens and blues and golds . . .

But it didn't heal properly, he goes on. We didn't have the proper medicine. So this is what I'm stuck with. He gives a little grin and runs his fingertip along the purple ridge.

Proud flesh, you tell him, remembering, still with some shame, your own after the twins' cesarean. The incision, grown infected, due to your depression and neglect. He likes that.

Proud flesh, he repeats. Yes, I *am* proud of it. It's a reminder of my underwater life—still in the sea mother, speared like a little fish. He looks at you, ardent again with thought. Green eyes ...

We *should* wear our scars proudly, don't you think? They're a map of where our souls have been.

Later, you'll remember to call home, check on the kids. Chaos as usual, your husband tells you. Your sister called. She said you'd called her, something about meeting up at the lake this weekend? No, you'll say. That was about another weekend. Oh. A silence. She said it turns out she could do it tomorrow night. I told her you were in Canada. Another silence. *Are* you in Canada? The whole conversation was really confusing. Yes, you tell him, Emma's easily confused. Don't worry about it, you'll work it out with her. Okay, he says. Another silence. Stupid, you think. Stupid ruse. "Sisters' night out." You'll have to call her again, concoct another lie. Aren't you going to tell him how things are going? Aren't you going to tell him where you are, what you're doing, who you're with, doing what with whom? Doesn't he have a little something to tell *you*? His voice comes back. Well. When you get home, we need to have a conversation. Yes, you'll tell him. Yes, we certainly do.

It has disturbed you, the phone call. The intrusion of "real" life on this other—whatever life this is. And what *are* you doing, having this, what shall we call it? A Mrs. Robinson's midlife fling? What are you looking for, Anya? What do you hope to happen? Is it sex? You don't even think so anymore. What then, just a little "platonic conversation?" That could have happened back in the cube. Though, speaking now of Plato, we're hardly talking here of anything remotely approaching the transcendent with this boy. Right? Nothing so metaphysically marvelous as the soul's reunion with its lost twin. Isn't that so? You can't honestly believe there'd be the slightest possibility of anything worth dying (or lying?) for. He's just an occasion for your curiosity to play. Just a mindless diversion, a little escape. A more-interesting-than-usual shell picked up on the shore of the Ocean of Unlikelihood, a brightly colored toy. Maybe that's the thing you're seeking. A splash of exotic color, of luster in a life gone so unutterably beige.

Still. It makes you a little disgusted. That it would come to this. Not a little indignant, too, at him for taking you on. Did he see it, something pathetic in your indecent little proposal? Poor affection-starved professor, all she needs is a little sun. Get her out in the open air, let her traipse around the cage, before shoving her back in her shadow-haunted skin. You bristle at any suggestion that this is charity. Yet look at yourself, Anya—what else would it be? Or is he playing you? Is this a trick? Some kind of conquest? You know it well, how college boys can be. Will he come back bragging to his roommates about how laughably far he led this rich bitch up the creek?

Or is that it? Is it money? Blackmail. Extortion. Will he threaten to make it public, threaten to ruin your family and job? He's of age, of course, but you don't fool yourself in thinking this little fling with an undergraduate would wash. Not with the press, the provost, the college president, not with the alumni magazine. You've heard of colleagues getting castrated for much less than this these days. And this is harassment, you're certain, in about the first degree. That little business about "getting to know you better for my letter"—a *hotel* room?—how much more blatant could an all-out proposition be?

Your family . . . That's another matter. For all its chaos, still, it is a *known* known (whatever that means). A functional dysfunctionality. A velvet cage, maintained by the genius-jailer, You-Know-Who. You hate to admit it, you want to gag at the admission, but what Emma said, it's true. Take him, the man, the star-studded architect, out of the equation, and—ding dong, Cinderella—it's through: the new house, new furniture, appliances, the 1,000-thread-count cotton sheets—they all go the time-immemorial way of the adulteress: boom—out on the street. Well. Not literally. You'd get an apartment. With your salary, a modest one at best. No benefits anymore for the merely Adjunct Whore. And the kids?

It's all too much. *What are you doing, Anya?* Through the kitchen window where you're standing in the dark, you locate his slender shadow on the dock. You finish uncorking the bottle of wine you've come to open. Ah, life. Should you go to him regardless, disrobe and stand for once as vulnerable and naked as the stars? Wouldn't you like to see where that sleek spear would take you? You close your eyes. You might dive through the peacock-colored depths and find yourself. You might meander through an eternal coral labyrinth and drown. Little fish, what is it, what is it really to enter the waters of another person's body? You lift the bottle to your lips, take a sip and shake the lake out of your head. No, Anya. No Adonis. That gorgeous orgy's just not going to happen.

You take your bags and make your way down the hall to your old room. You step inside, lock the door, cut the lights, undress, lie down—like you used to, on the bottom bunk, under Livvie. In the fishlight of the moon coming through the open curtain, you see the pale hills of your breasts rising and falling. In the valley of your belly, the forgotten sunken bed of the scar. Your fingers find it. Ah well. Wellaway. It was a good body once, you tell yourself and stroke toward sleep.

When you wake in the morning, the motorcycle will be gone.

II

Most things, it's been said, never happen. Most things remain in this room beyond our room, adrift in their worlds of unlived possibility like pickled embryos in squat, translucent jars (*The jars on jars lining your grandfather's shelves, the lifelong naturalist, in the lamplight of his study, his glass eye bent in memory over a luna moth's green wing. They don't eat, Anya, he told you. They're born without a mouth. They have one day to find a mate and breed. One day, to live one day, can you imagine that?*) . . . There are things you tell no one. There are nights you open the door to the other room and stand in the fishlight with the little jars of unlife, their tight pink hands and drowsy milky eyes. Blind eyes that gaze, your girlhood used to believe, on God. Kristof was one. Kristof, he comes to you, the boy, not a boy, from that other liquid life, that lake-life room beyond this lapping room, its walls rippling with summer moonlight. How long have you forgotten him now? How final the forgetfulness of even the shades themselves, those revenants wavering between the gates of horn and ivory. Listen. From the dock, there's the sound of lake water knocking against the side of a drawn canoe. *Knock. Knock.* Rise from the sunken bed, step through the fishlight, in the untime, down to the moonless drifting shore. No one's there. No one is waiting for you. Anya, unAnya. Rise and open the door.

The canoe will glide light beneath your hand (Look at Livvie), your paddle plashing soundless through the eddies of your strokes, strong strokes, firm and purposeful, as they never were in life. The shore behind you rises with pale hills—pale lines of smoke, rising from the glowing fires of longhouses where there's the smell of roasting venison and boar. O Seneca. Oas-in-in Ka. Whose name translates, you know from long ago, to Keepers of the Western Gate, right, Father? They of the Standing Stone.

He was a stone where he stood, staring into the obliterating blaze of sunset on the water, where the two of them would row. He was a stone at the end of the dock, upright, gazing into the starry heavens, to tell the names of constellations to a child, to you, you three in one, three sisters. A stone on his tongue, his eyes two small blue stones, after autumn closed the chamber of his heart

(But in my father's house are many chambers)

Kristof was one. The boy, not a boy, carving down the lake's imaginary shore, in a silver canoe beneath a canopy of summer foliage, in the green, green light, to meet you, singing. *My paddle's keen and bright, flashing with silver, follow the wild goose flight, dip and swing, dip and swing . . .* The boy from Geneva, on the lake's northern tip, a local—would he live there still? It's doubtful. You were both fifteen, that unlifetime ago, in the green, green light and lapping water.

Down in the forest
Deep in the lowlands
My heart cries out for thee
Hills of the North
Swift as a silver fish
Canoe of birch bark
Thy mighty waterways
Carry me forth

It was a song he sang, he who was always singing, since you heard it first, his voice, like an invisible silver thread spun out before you in the woods one day, on one of your motherless wanderings, in those deep and pensive solitary spells, God-wrecked, Godhaunted—

Though I am forced to flee
Far from my place of birth
I will return to thee
Hills of the North

High and clear, rinsing and ringing, how it drew you. It drew you. That, and the smell of woodsmoke coming, as you made your way closer, from the little cove, the inlet where you'd always come to sit, where you had come to sit since childhood. How many faeryboats of moss and birchbark had you launched from that sandy shore? How many voiceless longings uttered? It seemed to you then, in some mysterious way, he'd heard them, had materialized, and sallied forth.

But you didn't approach him. You kept your distance, watching him, hidden in the trees. Long, lanky arms; blonde, shaggy head of hair and shirtless in his faded '70s jeans, with a smiley-face PEACE patch on the back pocket, you remember. He'd made a little fire there on the beach, this boy, and was squatting on his hams beside it, holding a fish, a little trout he'd caught, speared on a stick.

(And later, as you sat beside that sunken fire and watched him floating in the water (but this, much later), belly-up, his sequined skin glimmering in the droplets of noonday sun, you who had never seen a boy's naked body, not till then, what was it that it seemed to you as you watched him bobbing there? A slender blade of light? The paddle blade he sang, dipping and swinging? In the green, rippling water, the blinding absence of it all, the sliver of an invisible opening door . . .)

Something was opening in you. That summer you approached, curious, stepping forward from the trees, surprised with this new ease with which you walked, as though it were another body. You felt your girlself watching you from the leaves behind, enfolded in the shadows of the foliage, too tentative to venture, but also curious as to what this newly sprouting self would do—with its lengthening limbs, breast-buds and trunk erect, striding forward—before she turned with gig-gles and blushes abashed and hurried off, disappearing in the trees. You approached, and it seemed to you he sensed you, for he didn't startle, didn't turn to look as you took your place beside him and sat down. He continued singing softly the song he'd started (*Blue lake and rocky shore*), and as the words ended, and it trailed off in a humming (*I will return once more*), it seemed to you you'd always sat, the two of you together there, looking into the little fire invisible in the sun, wordless, without a sound except the warm, familiar murmuring of the sandy shore before you, his canoe so strangely pulled upon it, knocking.

There was time, an infinite amount, it seemed, before you went to it. Time to sit and wonder at the new people sitting there, so strangely without a history, without even a past, just freshly emerged from the green trees and summer water.

And there was grace, in the breaking of that little meal of fishloaf that he gave, with a swallow of his elderberry wine. This boy, not fully anymore or less a boy, who'd found you, no longer what you previously had been—two voids, substantial now, not even strangers—though still and always evermore to each other to remain strange—there, at the cusp of something coming into being, which had come into being, and now the world felt changed.

That's it, Anya. For once, on one bright day, the world felt changed.

That's the fire you're striking out for now, through the nightsounds of a thousand loons and the rippling of your paddleblade through black water. Searching the coves and crannies where you kept your moonless vigil, those nights that you lit out to meet him, the cabin quiet, all asleep, with only Livvie knowing. (The lake smell in your hair when you returned, the fishsweet smell of him across your chest and limbs, climbing back in the bunk beneath her as the sky outside took on its first ghost whitenings—Anya, she'd whisper, isn't it good? Isn't it so good to be alive? And you'd lie there in the secret mystery of that, with the length of him, the long slim shape of him, lying still inside you, growing.)

Nothing has changed. That's what you tell yourself. A thousand years ago and still the sky flings up its milky wonders, replete with all unutterable stars. The things that never happen go on being what they are, they never dwindle into dawn's diminishment. All semen, the starry heavenwide, in the embryonic night (the milky jar) you can hold him still, you can hold anyone. It is not death exactly. Death is coming into being. It is all the life unbeen.

Still, you wonder why it so seduces you. Isn't your devotion to the living? O Seneca. Why do you return? Wasn't being, merely being once, enough?

And what if you'd flown with him that night, that final night, beside the failing fire, when he stood and pulled you to your feet and led you into the water? No going back, he said—and you knew he meant forever, that he was thinking of the flight, south and farther south, of the wild geese, those shadowsounds above the lake fog rolling in, low over the unseen water. You could lose yourself inside it, that milky cloak, you knew that; it had nothing anymore to do with time, with summer ending and the cabin being locked, who knew it now? for its eternal season. No. It was not time. Time was what you both were out of, as a canoe drawn out of water, the silver fish gathered from the shallows, breathing the killing air; you hung there, on the thin invisible thread of that wild moment, on a songline of blue smoke, the two of you, bright-eyed and dying. And the loon's

lost voice in the silver glimmering dark—the saddest, the loneliest-loveliest sound
you could imagine. Your heart like a bristling bear hearing the hunter. And the
loon, unseen, like a spearhead drifting, its red eyes set upon it.

You still could do that. You could choose to lose your life. You could wrap
yourself in the skin of the unbeen and fly, freefloat forever. It's only another form
of human sacrifice. In the things you tell no one (but Livvie knew), he's still
inside you. Little fish that leapt from the shallows one bright day, to the hollows
of your heart and caught. In a milky pool he rounds and rounds, never going
anywhere, never growing. Little Kristof. Little lonely unborn love. He may be,
Anya, the closest that you'll see to God.

A tap at the window returns you to yourself.

Blue lake, blue line of smoke, blue song, a shred of it, lingering still—
catch, catch—twining and tangling in the cochlea's shell-rich quiet. A
shred of it. The scar along your belly taut, itself somehow a silver song-
shred tingling *tap* with droplets of solder *tap* bright crescent the sutures
gleaming sap— What is it? *tap tap*

Time.

Gradually the other room recedes—the lapping bed, rocking boards
of a dock, the coral walls awash with moon-gill ripple. Aurora umbels
of bubbles effervesce. Splay. Dissipate . . . Some words.

You're here, in the hazy-grainy light (what century?), cocooned in
Egyptian 1,000-thread-count cotton. Cleopatra, damasked and laven-
dered, on her queen-sized burnished barge, drifting through gold dust
down the winding River Cydnus? No, Anya. Beiged. Unscented. Ithaca.
Just home, you hay-haired faeryhankering child. Just back in time.

In time you hear your husband breathing—reedy, adenoidal. In time you hear those padded little soles—soon now, soon now they'll rise and patter down the parquet thoroughfares of the vast suburban blankness of your mind. They're coming. It, all of it, another day, is coming, inconceivably. In time.

Still . . .

You turn your head to the window where, behind the pallid shade, you hear a light tap tapping. What is it? Rain? Wouldn't rain be fitting? A mealy autumn drizzle mirroring your brain, in the mama haze, off in some misty mountain jungle, with a manchimp playing Tarzan-Dick and Jane. While in Florida, you remember, in the mangroves of Sarasota, a houseboat reels in pickerel and gin. And the parents, two who should never have come together, are the infants, Emma, yet again.

He would have returned for you. (That's right, baby Anya, slip back into the skin of all seductive improbabilities.) He would have. He'd only gone for a morning ride. In the things you tell yourself, you can still hear his silver Triumph purring down the water's sunlit eastern side. He wouldn't have left you stranded, cordless phone in hand, pacing the dock in a wild-haired panic. And when he did, when he appeared at the end of the eternal dirt-road drive, puttered up to the porch, cut the engine and dismounted, smiled, you'd have found, inexplicably enough, that you were ready, you were ready, Anya, for him.

You'd have taken him by the hand and led him in. Down the hallway, to your childhood room, its tomb, that would be fitting, wouldn't it? your old bunk, forever under Livvie. In the imagined morning, with only one ghost watching, you'd have laid him down in the granular light, the curtain drawn against the unkindly flood of sun, for it was important to you somehow that he not see your body. You'd have opened your robe and drawn him close, skin to skin, scar to scar, like a child across your sunken, milkless breast, across the hollow of your heart, where your heart had one time been, and then you'd be at rest.

Isn't that what you wanted? (Isn't it, Anya? Isn't it good?) Heartless, Anya. At last. And the slow sifting of sister ashes falling across you overhead, erasing your shadowy forms, the soft, inconsequential swirl of flake on winter flake, as you held him still, as you held anyone. And the world would recede on soft Egyptian cotton. And the souls would rise, with other mouths to feed. And the tapping at the window? O Christ, for one bright day, O let it be something green. A luna moth, lost amid the dazzle of the morning.

I WILL LAY ME DOWN

The Concert in Central Park, the hugely celebrated, hugely attended reunion of folk-rock icons Paul Simon and Art Garfunkel after a decade's estrangement, took place on the evening of September 19, 1981. Early that morning, the crowds that would swell throughout the day to half a million people began to arrive, claiming places in the drizzling rain that, as if by some higher ordinance, stopped just as the concert started. The Mayor of New York City introduced the duo to a thundering avalanche of applause as the stage door opened and the stars stepped forward. Awe washes Garfunkel's still boyish face; Simon said later he didn't fully comprehend the magnitude of the event until after it was over, when he got home and saw the crowd—and themselves before it—on the television screen. The concert was recorded and released as a double album the next year, eventually going platinum; HBO bought the viewing rights and released a full-length film. It ranks as one of the largest crowds ever assembled for a concert in America.

They had been there, together, although they didn't know it. She had come mid-morning with a group of college friends and had secured a spot not too distant from the stage. He was farther back, to the right, under a stand of trees, near a section that had been blocked off for city planners. He had searched for her, both of them had, since. There's a moment at 00:52:40, during the song "Kodachrome," when the camera gives a view of the crowd from the stage and she had sworn that's where she had been standing—there, or some place very near. A woman sways in the foreground of the shot, holding an infant in a pink knit hat. Behind and around her, all goes dark; the video still bleeds out to a nebulous blur, a tantalizing, grainy facelessness.

He had bought the video last summer for their tenth anniversary. He thought it might be nice, after dinner, after the children had been put to bed, if they could sit on the sofa and watch it together. How that would please her, maybe. They could remember, from their separate distances and individual perspectives, how each of them had experienced the show, where they'd gone in their lives after, and how eventually they'd end up here, together, watching themselves watching them again. There was a story in that, he thought. Paul might even have used it for a song. Two people sitting on a sofa (like a park bench, like bookends), watching the video that erases them as strangers, contains them in the crowd, separate-yet-together, still anonymous to each other in the faceless dark. He thought she might like that. Everything still on the verge of happening. Everything, their lives together, suspended in potential.

The concert was the brainchild of then Park Commissioner Gordon Davis and New York City music promoter Ron Delsener. It had been planned as a much-needed benefit for the Park, which had fallen into chronic disrepair and neglect over the past twenty years. Once the glory of the City, Manhattan's "green lung" had become an untended, overgrown and crime-infested dump. Garbage proliferated; the great statues and fountains of the previous century had been defaced. Rapes and robberies made the place too dangerous to venture into at night. Equipped with a dwindling and beleaguered police force, the Mayor had even suggested permanently closing it down. It would require an estimated three million dollars to restore it to its former civic grandeur and to maintain it; a benefit concert was planned as the first step. Simon

and Garfunkel, both natives and lifelong residents of the City, who returned to it over and over in their songs, seemed to Delsener and Davis
the natural choice.

The video shows the two performers shaking hands before the first
song, "Mrs. Robinson," begins. It's an oddly stiff, businessman-like ges-
ture that seems to say, "All right, pal, let's put the past behind us." But as
the music starts, and the old familiar harmonies and melodies kick in,
a strange thing happens. It's as if no time at all has passed. It's 1969 all
over. The past is all there is.

+

He had come to the City in 1965 after finishing graduate school in
California. As a brilliant and innovative young architect, he'd been part
of a small team responsible for the reimagining of the World Trade
Center complex in lower Manhattan, close to Battery Park: a group of
seven buildings, it was proposed, that would replace the present single
structure, exponentially expanding its operations and scope, and ulti-
mately securing (if it had not already been secured in some primitive
pea of a brain on the other side of the planet) New York City's postwar
preeminence as the financial capital of the modern world. More, to his
mind, the complex would stand as a kind of matrix of ideas, or tangible
symbols, metaphor made concrete and titanium that, in the postmod-
ern style of the day, would bring the glories of antiquity into witty and
ironic play: truly *world* trade. The merchants of Phoenicia, the trades-
men of Constantinople, these were our contemporaries. By structural
cross-sectioning, a people remained visibly—synchronously—con-
nected to its historical plurality of culture, which is always happening
now, in an ever-streaming moment: history was accidental placement in
a continually accruing state of consciousness; there was never any more

history or reality than there was now. Architecture would be the sign, the visible manifestation of this synchrony; it would provide a static voyage for the mind as well as the body—in time-outside-of-time. Such were his thoughts. Such his small team of designers believed.

But dissatisfaction and disillusionment had set in with the rival design, and ultimate erection, of the infamous "Twin Towers." Unornamented file cabinets for interchangeable human bodies, he'd have called them; they violated every principle to which architecture in the present should aspire. Grotesque (not even *that*) gigantism, soulless hubris, a monumental failure. Worse than worst. If this was the future, as now apparently it was, an eyesore standing in perpetuity to mock him, he wanted none of it. In defeat and indignation, he left the firm and moved uptown to begin again, alone.

On the streets of West Harlem, in the vicinity of Columbia, he had wandered. In his mind he went back to the desert of his youth, that great basin east of the Sierra Nevada whose vacancies had filled him with dry sky. His mind dwelled in and among its crags and crevices; he revisited the cave he had discovered as a child, with its forgotten crate of dynamite and ornamental watermarks resembling bison. An ocean had once lain here. He thought of the stillness and silence of that ancient floor. He imagined himself a crustaceous eyeless creature inhabiting a conch's endless whorl. He lay for what seemed an eternal reverie, watching seasons pull and pass across the range in cloud-shadow cobalt, sage and lightning-tangle and, suddenly, a tumble of snow. Imageless adrift, his mind a mirror, and in him also emptiness. Parents and people, all attachments, ties, forgotten.

Maybe he should take her there, he thought. The family vacation he had planned for them, last summer in Niagara, had been disastrous. The twins had constantly fought, they never slept, were up at dawn; the shared family tent was the worst idea imaginable. They'd finally given up and checked into a hotel suite, where she'd lain in bed with the door locked for most of the last day, not even venturing out with them to see the Falls. No. He meant take *her* there, her alone—it had been so long since they'd been able to get away somewhere together. In the third-world hijacked bus (as she called it) their lives with these creatures had become.

But in the desert you could recover. You could climb back into your original skin. You could lie naked to the world under the unseeing eyes of the sky—. A memory came to him: he was riding out (was it 1959?) with a girl in his father's Alpha Romeo. She was the daughter of a neighbor; he'd known her all his life. The convertible top was down. And as they crested the mountains, without saying a word about it, they began to remove their clothes. First her, her top; then he, taking up the challenge, intrigued and curious about where all this would go. It was the summer after they'd both graduated high school.

He remembered feeling a kind of wonder at her body. That he'd known it so long, that it didn't belong to him, that it had changed really even without his noticing into a woman's. And as they coasted down the rain shadow, deeper into the starless basin, how it even—how *his*— took on a life of its own: the cooled ocean air blowing their nipples erect, his undisguised, undisguisable arousal. None of this was expected. Nothing of it had been predicted. It must have been the farthest thing from either of their minds. But now—*and* now—they were in it.

That was a nakedness he wished for her. Not hers, the girl's, not her younger, vibrant body; not the past, not anything that would never come again—but that condition of pure, spontaneous possibility where anything could happen. It *had* happened they'd made love—if that's what you want to call it—at the bottom, on the arid ice-age ocean floor, but that was beside the point. That was them, *their* story; that was the way it ended, their California childhood's valediction. For the two of *them* (he turned to her now in the passenger's seat where she was sleeping), what was the way it went? What was *their* story? Would they make it to the desert's other side? Would they even emerge together?

He had hoped things would be better after the move to Ithaca. The City really was no place to try to raise small children. Maybe for other people, maybe for people without these twins. It was too much; they couldn't be contained. The four hours they'd lost them at the Coney Island aquarium, that had sealed it for them. And she wanted to finally use her doctorate, not just see all that coursework and research wasted. Festering alone mindless in the apartment all day while he worked. "You'd better be very good," she'd said to him one evening, when he returned to find the place a wreck, the children covered in vegetable oil and screaming. Better be very good, was what she meant, to be so selfish.

So the move. The new house. Her position at the college that seemed (at least she'd told him) promising. The children getting older, going to school—it *was* better, it was getting better, wasn't it? Still. Whole evenings without talking, the two of them on opposite ends of the house. They'd just as well have been at opposite ends of a city block, still unknown to each other, still turning to their separate lives after the concert was over, into the black anonymous night outside the screen.

+

On the screen, the two singers rarely ever look at each other, almost never make eye contact, though Art watches Paul carefully for the phrasings of his new songs. There's little of enjoyment to be seen in Paul's performance. Expressionless, Picasso-like, he stares into the sway-ing void, feet planted, as if marking an invisible point on the hori-zon towards which his voice must navigate. It's Art who appears to be relishing the moment, his swinging arms, still boyish smile, marveling eyes that catch the floodlights overhead like flashing stars. Watching him sing, it's easy to believe he's recreating what it must have been first to sing those songs—to be first in the condition of being able to sing them—as they emerged like strange new birds from beneath Paul's fingers on the strings. That awe-filled, naked, original wonder. The third song in the set, "America," must have been one of those songs. When he finishes his solo of the perfect "April Come She Will," accompanied by Paul's lone acoustic guitar, Paul turns to him—for the first time in all the concert—and actually smiles. He puts his hand on Art's shoulder. You want to believe he's made Paul feel it, too. That original, that unadulterated sense of wonder.

When had *he* felt that first? When had she? When was the first time they, the two of them, felt it first together? He remembered once, early in their relationship, while making love, the mystery of their lying there together, how it was that they were lying there together, how out of all the unlikelihood of disparate ages, geographies and contorted city streets they had found each other, broke open freshly upon him. She was still really a stranger to him—they were strangers to each other, two people casually met over a smoky jukebox—but it seemed to him then, in that timeless after-time of a dangling conversation that could never be completed, it seemed to him that two vast spaces, two horizons, had converged and opened before them in a new conglomerate world. It was a world of pure potential they would realize: it would enter *their* world through her. He couldn't see the contours or the definition of it clearly, but he knew—he knew it in her younger, youthful form—it was there. It filled him with such an overwhelming sense of something beyond happiness—though happiness was there—and the boyish delight and curiosity and wonder at their bodies, seen it seemed as from above, as they strained and writhed and called to each other on the bed. He felt he could press forever and not reach the distances inside her, and he pressed and pressed. She was out there, on the horizon he imagined, beckoning. She was taking him into all they were becoming—into what would become *through* them—and it filled his heart with such a sense of—was it awe?—his eyes broke open into sudden tears. He held her then for all that he was worth. He held on to her naked body. It was the future now he saw he wasn't letting go.

And then: twins. Completely unpredicted, unforeseen. Little wonders. Their Niagara moment. The big, barreling fall.

He watched them helplessly and individually disintegrate as she withdrew into a razor-wired seclusion, the blank of her eyes, the gray of her expression a private, concrete cube. The irony, the precise symmetry of it, was of course perfectly cruel: they two had created the two that would destroy them. In their straining towards each other, they had produced the very strain that with its seismic force had shaken the foundations. The split egg: the atom, split. The Adam (he), the Anya (sleeping), in the Audi, driving through the dark, from a birthday concert in Syracuse back to dreamy Hiroshima. Homeward bound . . . In the year of our unmaking, 1995, having attained the unlikely age of fifty-three, have you anything but your annihilating offspring to declare? (he asks himself). He looked over at her, dreamless against the pane. I declare I loved you once unspeakably.

He turned his eyes quickly back to the wheel and shifted the Audi into a lower gear. One had to be careful on these icy roads. Stay alert, Adam. Stay awake. The drizzle that had begun some hours past had gathered now into a freezing rain. Inside the windshield wipers' *thunk thunk thunk* he could see the snow on the shoulder plowed high to the trees that arced above them, their branches sleeved with ice, a black canopy twinkling with the momentary gleam of their lights. They passed a car that had slid off into a snowbank. She murmured something in her sleep and stirred. No sign of a driver. The stalled headlights carved their twin golden tunnels through the steaming, seamless wall of white.

The cassette tape that had been playing had run itself out and had begun another loop. He considered reaching down to the floorboard for the carrying case that lay open at her feet. But no, it was too treacherous. He didn't want to risk waking her. And God knew she needed sleep. It was all right. He could listen to it again. It was "The Sound of Silence."

+

Rehearsals during the few weeks prior to the concert had been a miserable affair. The two had constantly fought. Paul had rewritten some of the lyrics to the old songs, which irritated Art to no end. He had envisioned singing them the way they'd always performed them, accompanied solely by Paul's acoustic guitar, but now Paul had rearranged them to accommodate synthesizers and horns and other instruments. It was too much. Old tensions began to resurface, adding vitriol and fuel to the newer ones. He had always felt himself inferior to Paul, to his accomplishment as a songwriter; Paul had long grown impatient with a partner who contributed little more than a choirboy's songbird tenor. Desiring true collaboration, he had gone off in search of larger bands, more vital, international influences.

A person would never know any of this, standing there. In that tremendous faceless wash, there is no place for bitterness, rancor, for anything other than the sense of living—of reliving—a singular American adventure. A momentous reunion, the coming together of two legendary voices, in perfected, reconstructed harmonies. Just as it was, just as it had always been. A grand thing to be able to witness, to remember. At one point, Paul says to the crowd, "They didn't allow us any fireworks.

So let's make our own." Five hundred thousand voices lift in a unified cheer as the lighters rise into the darkness and hang there through the last song, a swaying nebula of momentary stars.

He wanted to tell her they were still there and he himself believe it. He wanted to tell her it was going to be all right. Nothing was over, they'd just gotten a little lost. Something was searching them out in that darkness, something was bringing them together—it would happen, all of it would happen, given time. In a sense, looked at now, from this distance, it had *already* happened. They were the evidence, sitting there, in and outside the screen, watching the strangers through the years find each other again and again. What a reunion it would be if somehow, this time, they could only get it right. The future would happen, he thought, if they could just get to it in time.

Another car had slid off the highway into a tree. A patrol car was pulled up behind, its red and blue lights swirling in the cloud of rain and steam as they pulled slowly past. A man and a woman huddled in the momentary flashing, their faces drawn, hers beneath his jacket; the man was speaking to the policeman and pointing at something ahead. He glanced at the clock on the dash and readjusted his speed. Not long, he told himself. Stay alert. He rubbed his eyes and tightened his grip on the wheel. Soon. They'd be home soon.

He pictured the children tucked into their twin beds sleeping. Sweet dreams. Sweet dreams. When they got in, if she wanted, maybe he'd make a fire. It wasn't too late (he looked at the clock again). He'd lay a blanket down in front of it. Maybe she'd come to him, lay herself down, maybe she'd let him in again. He pictured her body on the morning they were born, so ravaged and emptied. He pictured her before it all began: the two of them, in a whitewashed office, when the OB/GYN announced: "Twins." Their faces, awash with disbelief and wordless wonder at what had found them, at what would be bringing itself to be through them. Was it possible? He closed his eyes and saw a semi coming, its headlights like horizontal towers in the night, barreling down, too fast now to avoid, the road too slick to swerve into the other lane. He opened them to a wall, an avalanche of white. Her face was in it somewhere, still vague, a little hazy, as if searching itself to recognize him. Adam? Wasn't he even going to say a single word?

No—, he said.

ABOUT THE AUTHOR

Todd Hearon has received a PEN/New England "Discovery" Award, the Friends of Literature Prize (*Poetry* magazine and the Poetry Foundation), the Rumi Prize in Poetry (*Arts & Letters*), the Campbell Corner Poetry Prize (Sarah Lawrence College), and the Paul Green Playwrights Prize (North Carolina Writers' Network). A Dobie-Paisano Fellow (University of Texas, Austin), he served as the Poet-in-Residence at Dartmouth College and the Frost Place. He lives and teaches in Exeter, New Hampshire.

CPSIA information can be obtained
at www.ICGtesting.com
Printed in the USA
BVHW031254150222
PP13161200001B/2